My Precious Pip

BY
KENNETH ASLANIAN-WILLIAMS

Copyright © 2013 by Kenneth Aslanian-Williams
All rights reserved.

ISBN: 1481915452
ISBN-13: 9781481915458

To veterans

Robyn,
Thank you for your interest and for your kind words re: my first book (Quiet Shelter).

Kent Ashe-Well

GRATITUDE

Thank you, **Susan Jacobson**, for devoting a substantial portion of your life over the past twenty years to reading my work. Thank you for the courageously harsh criticism and for the unstinting willingness to read the same material again and again. And again.

Thank you, **Eli Hall**, for reading so carefully and editing so keenly, for criticizing and encouraging in perfect proportion (90/10).

Thank you, **Dr. Amy Hecht**, for reading so much of my work with a physician's eye for medical detail.

Dottie

My wife Dottie died last year, 2007. September fifteenth, in our bed, in my arms. She was eighty-one. I died that day too but I didn't know it at the time. I continued to live in our home, a lovely two-story traditional with a few Art Deco touches on Paloma Street, a quiet patch of residential civility in the western reaches of San Francisco. Dottie had made it a lovely home for thirty-seven years. It wasn't so lovely after five months of widower-hood. I fired the cleaning lady in the second week – I couldn't bear another woman handling things around the house. Some time in the third week I stopped washing the dishes. I stopped paying the gardener in the second month and in the third month he stopped coming. I never changed the sheet that Dottie had died on. I just couldn't. The imprint of her body was so distinct. It seemed a tangible promise of her return to me, like she had gotten up to go to the bathroom and would be back in a minute or so.

Every day of those five months I would wake up and ask myself why I continued to live, why I would do that to myself. These were clinical questions, not rhetorical ones of self-pity. No answers came to me, no resolution to change my status in any way. I marked it down to lethargy rather than cowardice.

The mail. I stopped looking at it the day I returned from Dottie's funeral. I hated the very sound of the postman pushing it through the mail slot in our front door. It was like the outside world beckoning me to get back on some sort of hamster wheel: shop and spend until I die. Everyday I would just push it into the corner beside the door with my foot. By the third month it was a mountain. In the fourth month, I just scooped it all up and dumped it in the recycling bin. Thank God my pension payments were auto-deposited to a bank account and my utility bills were paid through automatic debits. Thank God for Dottie: that was all her doing.

We were childhood sweethearts, from Indiana. We met in the spring of 1940 when her father was driving his family to a wedding and his car broke down with her in it. He had to push the car half a mile to my father's repair garage. When she came out the back of that car in that pink chiffon dress I stopped breathing for whole minutes. When I managed to inhale again it was someone else in my old body. That someone else had feelings and interior edges that cut into my fifteen-year-old flesh from the inside out. Dottie didn't tell me until our fifth wedding anniversary that she had had similar feelings when she got out of the car and saw me staring too long at her.

We were so innocent in our heat. We kissed a lot when the theater lights went down and that was about it. One time, standing on her porch enjoying a good night smooch, my hand wandered down to her behind. She didn't speak to me for two weeks.

But the night before I left for Virginia to be shipped overseas, she offered me everything. She said she knew of this hotel, in the Negro part of town, but clean. The front desk people were sympathetic to couples about to be broken up by the war. You literally just walked in and told them that you were shipping out to fight Hitler and they just handed you a room key. I didn't think to ask her how she knew all that until we had been married twenty years. But back then, in 1943, I was just boiling with the dilemma: I wanted her so much but I just didn't think that was fair. She might get pregnant and I might not come back. Or I might come back a cripple. But I made it back in one piece. Physically anyway.

We were married in November 1945. She was nineteen; I was twenty. We had two children, a boy and a girl. The boy, Brad, arrived in 1948. He was smart enough to skip a grade and graduate high school at seventeen. He went to West Point, graduated near the top of his class despite his relative youth and launched what promised to be an utterly brilliant career. Our girl Melissa just never got her feet under her. She was born colicky and just stayed restless. Throughout her adolescence she moved from one adventure to another, the "adventures" usually involving boys, and then men, much older than she. Melissa moved out of our house when she was sixteen, went to live in some sort of communal house in Haight-Ashbury.

One day Melissa comes to our house and drops off her child, asks us to watch her for "a week or two." She was headed to Woodstock, she said. No one she knew would be in town to take care of her child; they were all going to Woodstock. We had no idea what that was at the time. She never came back. We found out that she overdosed in a motel room in Pennsylvania on her way home. Melissa's companions confirmed all of this. They insisted on having a new-age funeral celebration. They would cremate her on what they called "a druidic pyre of love and farewell." We were too heartbroken to resist that silliness. They ended up half-burning her and abandoning their mess. We had to clean all that up. I mark Dottie's spiritual decline from that point. It was further accelerated by Brad's death in Vietnam in 1972. He was within six weeks of coming home safely. He was all of twenty-four.

We concentrated on rearing Melissa's lovely child Charmaine. She was a gorgeous little thing. She became our life, our only justification for laughing and planning with any sense of purpose or optimism. Joy turned to worry when Charmaine reached her teenage years. She had inherited her mother's sense of adventure and her lack of self-control. We couldn't keep up with Charmaine, didn't understand her (as she never tired of reminding us).

After a rough adolescence, Charmaine managed to graduate from high school, Abraham Lincoln in the Sunset District. She continued living with us as she attended San Francisco State, a half-mile down the street from Paloma. One day she walks in, says she's had enough of us and just leaves. I forget now how old she was at the time, but Dottie and I were in our sixties. We were exhausted, discouraged. Fortunately Charmaine was a bright girl and managed to complete a pretty decent education. The details of it escape me now. She had enough sense of herself to hang on to a man who married her and held down a job. So we thought at the time. But she let him slip through her fingers after a year of marriage. Then she herself just slipped out of our lives.

In 1994, out of the clear blue, Charmaine calls us and announces that she just recently remarried. She lives in Mill Valley now, a few minutes' drive across the Golden Gate Bridge, and she wants to invite us to the christening of her newborn baby. We didn't ask about the timing of those two events, marriage and birth. We were just glad to hear from her, glad that she wanted us back in her life and was reaching out to us. We went to the christening. A loud vigorous baby boy they named Ulrich. The father seemed a bit of an ass. Well, a real ass actually. At the christening lunch I caught him swiping his hand over the backside of this hot little thing with whom he claimed to have a close work connection. She laughingly batted the hand away, like she wanted to control the context but encourage the impulse. I didn't say anything of course.

Several months later Charmaine invited us to Thanksgiving dinner at their house. She and her husband were smilingly polite with each other and, other than their joint carving of the turkey, avoided each other like the plague. Dottie noticed too. In the car home she fretted so much that she was in tears by the time we pulled into our driveway.

Over the next several years we sent letters and cards to Charmaine and birthday gifts to Ulrich. We invited them to our house for Thanksgiving and Fourth of July, but Charmaine never responded. We never got together. One time we ran into them in Union Square during the Christmas shopping season. Charmaine and her husband seemed very happy and Charmaine was pregnant again. Ulrich was a really good-looking kid, a rather Viking looking guy with flaxen hair and these terrifyingly alert and adult-like eyes. Charmaine was quick to tell us that he had walked really early, talked really early and had a knack for numbers and concepts. Dottie wanted to steal him right then and there. She volunteered great grandmotherly baby-sitting services whenever Charmaine needed them. We made them promise to spend a weekend with us in Sea Ranch or Carmel. They seemed to be just as enthusiastic but they always had excuses when we followed up with specific dates. After a year we stopped trying. By the time Dottie died, we had been down to an annual exchange of Christmas cards for years. Dottie always ended our greeting with a *Let's get together in ____.* *Oh, please!*

Dottie and I were married sixty-two years. She was my life. In my grief I lost my appetite, and when I recovered it I quickly tired of food-shopping, cooking, and watching those unwashed dishes pile up like ceramic pyramids in the kitchen sink. I had my music but I found that I would often get through an entire Mahler or Bruckner symphony without having heard a note.

Why did I continue to live?

The question kept coming but not the answer.

I wasn't about to kill myself but I did go on some sort of a death watch. Even as I write this I'm not sure what that means, or what it meant at the time. I just knew that life as I wanted to live it was over and there was no need either to find a new purpose to life or to rush along toward the end. Just sit, listen to good music, pick up a good book now and then (I never finished them), go to movies. Wait.

But that house. Those carpets. Those dishes. Dottie was such a housekeeper. She kept our place spotless and perfect without ever giving the impression that she was a neurotic clean-freak.

All in all, March of 2008 just seemed a good time to exit from life in the larger world, to settle into three-meals-a-day at the Argyll Retirement Community in San Francisco where maid-service vacuumed and dusted twice-weekly and changed my sheets every Friday. Average life expectancy for a widowed Caucasian American male of middle class lifestyle: seventy-six or so. Me at the time: nearly eighty-three. Surely I wouldn't have long to wait. Perhaps a few years of boring tranquility before a curtain of dementia or renal failure dropped down on me.

The move to the Argyll was so easy. There was little in the way of household goods that I wanted to keep. I had haulers come and clear out the whole basement and garage in one clean sweep. I sold the mortgage-free house pretty much at the peak of the San Francisco real estate boom in the spring of 2008. I sold the Volvo and the cherried-out 1949 Packard which I kept shrouded in the garage and never drove. That Packard had been the first new car of our married life. Some young-kid internet billionaire drove all the way up from Los Altos Hills to check it out and plop down eighty-five thousand cash for it.

I bought a thousand-square-foot one-bedroom apartment in the Argyll Tower for cash and put a million in CD's. Yes, San Francisco homes are worth that much these days – ridiculous. I used the kid's eighty-five thousand to make a huge quarterly tax payment to keep Uncle Sam off my back; and arranged to have my army, school teacher and social security pensions auto-deposited in my new bank account at a Citibank branch down the street. I settled in to take long naps in my spotless living room, listen to my music, go to matinees at the Kabuki down the street in Japantown, attend evening movies in the intimate little 20-seat Argyll cinema, think my loving thoughts of Dottie and wait for death.

Mary: Oh, God

"Hi there," a voice behind me says. Before I can turn around a lovely sweet-scented woman is pulling out a chair beside me. Her startlingly clear blue eyes seem to fill the room. "You're new here, aren't you?"

"Yes, I am. I'm Morton Willbanks."

"Well, I'm Mary Givens," she says, sticking out a hand. It's a large long-fingered hand with close-cropped nails. It's just gorgeous: veiny to be sure but free of liver spots and that thin rice-paper look that old hands get. It takes me a few heartbeats to grasp the hand. It's warm.

"I'm in 912," she says, scooting up her chair.

"Very pleased to meet you," I manage to get out. "I'm in 510."

"Normally I would have greeted you as you arrived here. I'm chairwoman of our welcoming committee. But I've been on vacation for the past month. In Scandinavia, visiting my son. Are you a native Californian?"

My head whirls. I've heard about a third of what she's said. I've been lost in those eyes.

She asked...

"Oh. No. I...I'm from Indiana originally." I stutter – actually stutter like a pubescent kid exposed to my first pretty school teacher. I'm instantly embarrassed and guilty. A woman hasn't made me stutter since Dottie put me through my paces as I tried to convince her to go on that first date.

"Well, Mortie, welcome, belatedly, to the Argyll," Mary says intimately. "It's just great here – you'll love it. Are you here with your wife?"

"No, widowed," I mumble.

"Ah," she says knowingly on a half-sigh. "How long?"

"Nearly seven months now."

"God bless you." She breaks slowly into a mischievous smile, brushing back her fine silver hair which seems that way by choice and style and not by necessity of age. "Let me guess here: *She* did all the chopping, dicing, slicing, cooking and dish-washing, didn't she?"

God, does that ever sound sacrilegious. But I feel my overly-warm face smiling back at her.

"Yeah," I say. "Best cook in the world. Best baker too."

Mary's eyes sweep over me frankly, like she's measuring me for a suit or something. "Well, it's clear you've missed a few meals in the past seven months. We'll fatten you up here soon enough. Food's great here. I mean really great."

"Just ten days here has convinced me of that."

"Are you a veteran?"

I am stunned, like she's reached inside my chest and pulled out my most protected secret.

"I am. How do you know that?"

She shrugs. "It's a reasonable question to ask an American male in his eighties."

Eighties. Looking into her clear bright eyes I feel twice that age.

"ETO, PTO…?" she says.

"ETO," I say. "Normandy and onward."

Her eyes flutter for just an instant. When they settle, her whole face is more intimate and I think just a little vulnerable. "God bless you for your service," she says quietly. "I mean it. I was a German war orphan. It's a GI like you who saved me in 1945. A few years older than you maybe. He and his wife adopted me, took me back to Dayton, Ohio and gave me a wonderful life."

I want to apologize to her for any pain and dislocation which has ever visited her life. I feel devoted to her wellbeing in some stupid way and then I think of Dottie and sneer inwardly at myself.

"I'd love to join you for lunch today," she says, "but I've got a quarterly homeowner's association board meeting over there in two minutes." She nods in the direction of two men and two women sitting at a big round table across the dining room. They look expectantly in her direction. "You and I should have dinner soon. I'll introduce you to a couple of Argyll characters whom I'm *sure* my fellows on the welcoming committee steered you away from." She says this with a conspiratorial wink. "We're going to have fun."

"That sounds great."

"Take care, Mortie."

She rises gracefully but carefully, like an old dancer who is in great shape but who is not quite sure of her ankles. She smiles down on me and walks off. It is only then that I appreciate her height: five-eight easily, even without her heels which seem a little too high and sexy for that time of day, if not for her age which I still can't divine but guess to be mid-sixties or so based on her comment about her war-orphan status. I stare overlong at the back of her walking away. Trim figure, really nice legs. No stockings. No red splotches on her muscular calves. I think of Dottie's legs in her seventies and I want to slap myself. *Seven months, you fool. Who the hell are you anyway?*

Mortie.

That's who I am. I'm Mortie. No one had ever called me that. I had been Mo-Mo to Dottie ever since our lovemaking that night in the Negro hotel and I had remained Mo-Mo to her for six wonderful decades. I had been Mortar to my army buddies – I was good at aiming the squad's mortar tube. I had been Morton or Mort to my civilian world all my life. Now, Mortie!

I feel branded, like Mary Givens has marked me exclusively for her future use. I feel a little warmer in every one of my arthritic joints. *Seven months. You are eighty-something. You're hopeless.*

It turns out that Mary Givens is one of the most active residents in the Argyll. She's on several Argyll committees: the welcoming committee, the library committee, the menu committee. She's a docent at the de Young Museum and does suicide prevention work at a halfway house for what she calls TAGS -- thrown-away girls. But she keeps her promise to have dinner with me. Several times as a matter of fact. She shows me around the social landscape of the place, introduces me to a couple of her female friends who seem a little bit too lively for an old folks' home and who get downright wild with Mary when the three of them share a bottle of wine at dinner time. She takes me on three walks. The first is around nearby Japantown, to show me the best noodle and sushi places, to introduce me to two green grocers. The second walk is along upper Fillmore Street, which is white, affluent and bustling. The third walk is along lower Fillmore Street, which is black, struggling and depressing.

Mary laughs when she notices my discomfort during our first block on the lower Fillmore. There isn't a white person in sight.

"Get over it," she says lightly but seriously. "Life is going on here like it's not going on anywhere else in this city. It doesn't look like much now but give it a couple of years."

A couple of years.

I remember that I'm on something of a death watch and expect to be gone within a couple of years. Then I remember: I'm out in the world, aren't I? Exploring. Outside my comfort zone. Looking dark strangers in the eye. On something of a date with a lovely woman. I think of Dottie, of course. My confusion mounts but not my guilt.

"This is going to be the new Yoshi's," she says as we pass a building under construction. "It opens in November."

"What's Yoshi's?" I say.

She gives me a double take, like she's not sure I'm kidding. "It's the Bay Area's premiere jazz club. Started in Berkeley, moved to Oakland, is opening a second club here as part of the lower Fillmore's revitalization. I thought you loved music."

"Classical," I say defensively.

"Gotta work on that," she says smiling. She squeezes my forearm. "It might be time to stretch a little – never too late to stretch." Intimately she adds, "We'll come to Yoshi's several times."

We. I wonder if that's a you-and-me *we* or an Argyll Social Evening *we* where ten to twenty of the more active among us are herded into vans and taken out for a night on the town. An image rises in my mind of Mary's backside as she pushes herself up into a van. I kill that image quickly when Dottie laughs.

A lot of other images in my brain become a lot more heated. My nightmares become much more complicated. The usual montage of my buddies' ripped bodies and agonized faces is, more nights than not, interrupted here and there by a still image of Mary's face. One night I start to instant wakefulness by the sight of her lips moving right toward me. I can't be sure when I awake, but I think she was naked. I am covered in the usual sweat but I laugh.

I start taking a great deal more care with my appearance. I start wearing a wrinkle-free sports jacket and a silk tie to evening meals. I begin to lament the continuing loss of my fine hair and when an old-age ulcer erupts on the back of my hand I curse it and cover it with a band-aid.

"What happened to your hand?" Mary asks the very next morning after I've slapped on the first of many band-aids.

"Cut myself," I mutter. "Slicing and dicing all those fruits and vegetables you got me."

She laughs and squeezes my good hand. Jesus, she is such a great squeezer.

"I should have known better," she says. "I should have given you a few lessons on how to navigate a kitchen without killing yourself." She pats my hand now. "Not too late I suppose."

"Yes, let's do that soon," I say.

I immediately feel so guilty because I immediately think of the dozens of times in our first years of marriage that Dottie tried to get me involved in kitchen work. Simple stuff: bread veal, fry fish, wash lettuce. Any mindless little thing to keep me in the kitchen while she was working. To keep her company, to talk to her, to listen to her.

One day Mary takes me to the Walgreen's around the corner from the Argyll.

"We all shop here for day-to-day necessities," she says as we enter. "The low-fat milk is fresher here than in Japantown and this is the best pharmacy in town. They stock Depends in six different sizes and they never run out."

Ugh.

She senses my reaction without even turning her head to look at me. "Not there yet?" she says laughing.

"Not quite."

"Well, aisle three when you're ready."

She introduces me to the entire daytime staff at Walgreen's. They all know her. Every male gets this strange blank-eyed glow to him as she lightly touches his arm and pulls him into a circle of introduction with me.

"Howie, this is Mortie Willbanks, one of our new Argyll residents. I want you to take good care of him when he comes in here."

"Jimmie, this is Mortie Willbanks, one of our new Argyll residents. I want you to…"

"Billy, this is Mortie Willbanks, one of our new Argyll residents. He fought in France just like your grandfather and great uncle. I want you to…"

Each man nods with this goofy smile, his glistening eyes more on her than on me. Every man seems to accept his assigned familiar name as a badge of intimacy and seems honored to wear it, even the pharmacist's pimply-faced assistant. I know those looks on their faces. I'm sure that I look that way when she introduces me around the Argyll. We are a happy herd, free-ranging bulls in the pastures of Mary Givens' world.

But there is no romance in any of this, at least not from her side. I soon discover that I myself was never on her radar screen in that sense. She likes much younger men. Fifties, even late thirties. And she has them by the bushel. They accompany her on our Argyll evenings to Italian-style banquets in North Beach, to the symphony, to musical outings at The Rrazz Room. She and her man-for-the-evening actively participate in the Argyll outing and then melt into the night as the rest of us are re-boarding the Argyll vans. She often brings them to the dining room on nights when the menu promises an especially scrumptious meal. Then she goes out with them for the evening or simply walks them up to her apartment. A couple of times when I return to the Argyll after an early-morning walk (an old military habit never broken), I see one of her prior-evening dates leaving as I'm walking in. He looks grateful, humbled, privileged. Jealousy wells in me every time. I think of Dottie to tamp it down.

Mary Givens is quite open about it. Everyone knows. She carries it off though with great poise and dignity, like she has a right to live like a middle-aged Parisienne in the full blow of her second sexual wind. Some women hate her, many try to ostracize her. But her charm and evident affection for people draw most to her. Every time I have a chance to ask her why in the world she's at the Argyll at all with all her health and vitality, I just get lost in her eyes or paralyzed by that mischievous smile.

The only exception in her younger-men world is an eighty-something widower living on the second floor. He's in serious decline and seems utterly incapable of doing anything romantically, but she seems to care for him very much. They often sit at the far end of the community room, where no one can overhear them, and have long quiet conversations. He is also a German-born naturalized American. Strange though: they never eat together but they are always very conscious of each other when they sit apart in the dining room. I see her stealing glances at him even when she's involved with her nutty girlfriends. I catch him looking in her direction when he wipes his mouth or takes a sip of wine. I think to myself: Lord, if *he* has ever had any sort of a chance with her, then I –

I always cut myself off right at that point. Or rather, Dottie does.

I'm relieved, actually, that Mary has no romantic interest in me, that I don't qualify because of age. That reminds me that I *am* old, that I lack a certain appetite for life, an eye for opportunities -- that I'm on a death watch and that I'd best stick to it.

Mortie, though. God.

Charmaine Again

It's early May. I'm in the second month of my Argyll death watch when Charmaine calls me out of the blue. Her ex-husband (*ex* now) has fallen *back* into cocaine addiction and has begun missing alimony and child support payments *again*. Not having heard a real word from her in ten years, I didn't know that she had divorced and had no idea that her ex-husband had ever had a drug problem. She lives in Hayward now, in a duplex not far from the Hayward BART station. I know the Bay Area pretty well. I can envision the part of Hayward in which she lives and I divine that she has come down pretty far in the world.

She talks to me as though we've been chatting daily since she was old enough to talk.

Her childcare arrangements for the coming summer have fallen through, she says. Those arrangements were going to be barely affordable. Now she absolutely cannot afford the alternatives without the alimony and child-support payments. She dare not take even a minute off from this great new job she has secured with a company in the South Beach area of San Francisco. It's a gaming software company with young bosses who are single and childless and who have no sympathy for, or even the most basic understanding of, conscientious parents. Missing half a day here and there for childcare would surely get her fired and she would be replaced by a hyperactive over-educated twenty-something who has no children, no personal life to speak of, and who will be only too glad to work fifteen hours a day, six days a week.

That's the way Charmaine presents her situation: all in a breathless rush full of crisis and devoid of pauses or modulation, all in such intimate detail as if we two were the closest of relatives and I had been enmeshed in her life for the past decade. That was pretty much the way I recall her living the first two decades of her life with Dottie and me: as a never-ending crisis full of people who had let her down or were putting her under great stress.

"Can you help me here, granddad?" she pleads. "Just for the summer. I'll figure out something by the beginning of the school year. I really need you until then." She has no one else to turn to, she says.

I sigh – to myself, not into her ear. I'm on a death watch, I remind myself. The last thing I want clogging up my process is a weekly round of baby sitting.

"I don't cook anymore," I say, as if I ever had. "And I'm not sure a young child would like the food here." It's a lie. The Argyll's Saturday dinners and Sunday brunches are taken up with young kids gobbling down great food with grandma and grandpa. It's a weekly ritual.

Charmaine is silent for a long, long moment. During the silence I remember the times when she was fourteen or fifteen and she asked me if she could go out, the times when I said no you can't, when she'd just stand there with a hitched hip and her head cocked to one side, looking at me as if she were waiting for me to recover from a bad sneezing spell after which I would surely regain my senses and give her the only reasonable answer to her request.

"What does Ulrich like to eat these days?" I ask, just to break the silence.

More silence now. But the quality of it is very different: it's thicker, more freighted with something I can't divine.

"Hello?" I finally say, thinking the line has gone dead.

"Ulrich is dead, granddad. He died last year."

"What!" I virtually scream.

"I'm sorry – I thought you knew."

Why in hell would I know that? I want to shout at her.

"This is my second child you'd be watching. She's nine now. She won't be a minute's trouble to you."

I'm still stuck on *Ulrich is dead.*

"Honey, I am so sorry. I didn't –"

"An aneurysm," she says loudly, talking right over my condolences. "Very rare in a child Ulrich's age. He was twelve. We didn't even know he had it until…" Her voice trails off.

"Oh, honey, I am so –"

"We've moved past all that, really we have, yes, we have," Charmaine says in a rush. "We've processed our grief and we continue to hold him in our hearts and to celebrate Ulrich's time on earth and we're moving on."

It dawns on me that she doesn't even know about Dottie, that she hasn't asked how Dottie is doing. I conjure up an image of loving patient fifty-year-old Dottie staying up all night with one of Charmaine's many childhood ear aches.

"Pip is her name," Charmaine says. "She's a sweet girl. She's nine with a twenty-year-old intellect. I swear: you won't be talking kiddie-babble with this one."

And onward Charmaine rushes, as if she were a telemarketer with just twenty more seconds to hook me into her product. Pip is so mature, so self-sufficient, she says again; I won't even know she's in my space, she assures me; all I have to do is feed her breakfast and forget her until lunchtime, then feed her lunch and forget her until dinner time, then feed her dinner and forget her until Charmaine picks her up at some time around eight-thirty or nine.

"That late?" I say distressed, for myself and for a poor neglected nine-year-old girl bereft of her older brother.

"I work really long hours on Tuesdays and Thursdays. That's why I need you those days especially. Can you take her Tuesdays and Thursdays at least?"

I can't recall the day-to-day details of my early fatherhood, but I vaguely recall children of single-digit age being incredibly messy and dangerously energetic. I feel run-down already.

"How did she get the name Pip?" I ask, just to open up a little conversational space while I craft the phrasing for an excuse.

Pip isn't her real name, Charmaine tells me. Amani is her legal first name and Safari is her legal middle name.

Yes, that's right: the girl's American birth certificate reads *Amani Safari Carpenter.* Amani Safari is Swahili for *Peaceful Journey,*

Charmaine tells me proudly. She's now over a minute into her telephone spiel and I am thoroughly hooked. Something tells me that I should be more than a little distressed for this great grand daughter of mine whom I have never met.

Charmaine had given Pip that name at the start of her second trimester, when she was still so confident that her African lover was her baby-daddy and wanted to imbue the child with the physical power and spiritual strength of the whole African continent. Her words essentially, not mine. I don't ask how the Mandingo lover meshed with the marriage. Anyway, later, when it became clear at Pip's birth that the baby-daddy was actually Charmaine's own husband, she resolved to keep Pip's Swahili name as her formal legal name, figuring that it was plain bad karma to jettison a name with which Pip had already lived for two trimesters in the womb and by which Charmaine had called her during all of her pre-birth prayers and meditations.

Charmaine goes on and on and all I can think is: *Pip* for Chrissakes!

A boy's name. Not even a real boy but a literary boy. A Dickens character whom failed schools and the video/internet world had conspired to make more obscure and more irrelevant by the day. As a student and former teacher of language I eavesdrop on lots of conversations. I can't recall the last time I've heard anyone make reference to *Great Expectations* or even use "Dickens" in a coherent sentence. (Which reminds me: no one ever says anymore, "That scared the Dickens out of me." Today it's: "That sacred the living shit out of me." Or: "That scared the fucking shit out of me." More than enough said there.)

Pip. Good Lord.

Given all that I hear from Charmaine, it is quite evident that it is Pip I would be helping for the summer. I'm on a death watch, aren't I? What else had I to do with time that I don't really value? *I've got no one else, granddad. I could really use your help here.*

"Wait a minute," I burst in sudden revelation, "it's early May. Doesn't Pip have another month of school?"

A short silence.

"I had to pull her out of school," Charmaine says quietly. "She was having emotional issues at school." I think I hear her choke back emotion. "Never mind," she says with sudden poise. "Never mind, granddad – I can make it work."

"No, no, wait," I say. I'm thinking frantically now. I'm trying to rewire my brain in a matter of seconds to put myself in a place where I can be helpful to her without driving myself crazy. A troubled nine-year-old grieving over a dead brother? I'm eighty-three, I've got a weak heart, I'm tired, I'm grieving too in a way. I hear Dottie – she's trying to get in her two cents' worth – but I push her back.

"Let's take it a step at a time," I hear myself say. "Let's go with Thursdays for a while and see how things work out. You can make other arrangements for Wednesday through Friday, you say?"

I hear Charmaine's disappointment in the silence.

"All right," she says, her tone laced with mild censure. "We'll be there Thursday. I need to be in South Beach by seven-thirty. So, we'll be there by seven."

"Thursday," I say emphatically.

We hang up. I immediately want to call her back and give her my address and some basic driving directions. It dawns on me that she already has all that. She has my telephone number, doesn't she? How long has she had it – how long has she known where I live and just plain didn't give a damn? I simmer a little. I think of the times she made Dottie cry, the times Dottie and I stayed up to all hours waiting for Charmaine to come home, worried out of my minds. I remember the time she sits at the dinner table and announces by-the-way that she was pregnant up until last week. Up until *last week!*

Dottie hushes me indignantly. I see so clearly this image of her kind eyes, of her putting a finger up to her lips to quiet my welling anger over something Melissa or Charmaine had done. God, how many times she had had to do that in our years together.

Whatever Charmaine has become, she is ours again, Dottie whispers to me. *And Pip is ours. Now be grateful for that and stop your fussing.*

Pip

"Good morning, Mr. Willbanks!" Olga says with her usual high-octane cheeriness. "How are you this fine morning?"

"I'm just fine, Olga," I say, my voice warbling with dread and exhilaration.

"Your granddaughter Charmaine and your *lovely* great granddaughter Pip are here to see you. Shall I send them up?"

"Yes, please," I manage to get out.

"Fine. They're coming up now!"

I click off. As fast as octogenarian legs allow, I pace frantically around my little entry area. I debate whether to go out and meet them at the elevator or to stand on the threshold of my open door or to just stand inside my closed door and wait for the knock. But my lungs decide for me when they kick in again and I gasp for air. I've been holding my breath for the better part of a half-minute without knowing it and now I'm in no condition to do anything other than lean into the back of my door and snatch at my heart.

From the other side of the door I hear the muted ding-ding of the elevator in the lobby down the hall. I think again of Dottie and the hundred times we waited up to all hours of the morning, hoping and praying that Charmaine would make it home safe and sober. Resentment wells in me. Bitterness.

I hear an urgently whispering adult voice just the other side of the door. A tentative knock. I inhale deeply, exhale deeply and open the door to them. Charmaine's big doe eyes fill up my vision. They are not warm with reunion; they are all urgency and frustration.

"Hi, granddad – we are so late. This is Pip. Pip, this is your great granddad, great granddad Morton. Can you say 'hello,' hon?"

"Hello," Pip says cautiously with a tiny but confident voice.

"Hello, Pip," I say warmly. "Come on in, you two."

They both cross my threshold reluctantly, Charmaine as if she's entering an execution chamber.

Pip is a small thing. She has her mother's huge brilliant eyes and they seem to take up most of her little face. She wears a corduroy smock with shoulder straps that are wider than her skinny arms. The smock is an electrified fuchsia and hits her at her shins. She hugs this huge cardboard box which is as long as her own torso -- she clutches it urgently as if it's an airline flotation cushion and she's floundering in deep water. Her socks are mismatched in every conceivable way: one is long, bright red and cotton; the other is short, striped yellow-blue and wool. The socks form an eye-wrenching ensemble with her pink high-top sneakers. Her hair is short and disheveled -- for the briefest of seconds I think that I see something crawling in it but I quickly convince myself that this is my old man's imagination prejudiced by my revulsion over the girl's general off-putting appearance.

Pip and I are given no additional time for introduction. Charmaine fills the airwaves with complaints of her impossible day already getting away from her, with her fears that she'll get fired for being so late, with her need to leave right away to beat the cross-town traffic heading to South Beach. No acknowledgement of the time and distance that we have allowed to yawn between us. No, *how have you been the last ten years?* Still no mention of Dottie.

"This is great of you, granddad," the now breathless Charmaine says flatly as she finally realizes that she is still clutching Pip's backpack and puts it down just inside my door. "I didn't pack a lunch or anything. I'm sure the food here will be just fine."

"Sure," I say.

"Pip won't give you a minute's trouble," Charmaine assures me, one of her shoulders already pointing toward the door. "She's brought her favorite game: Axis and Allies. Ulrich taught her to play it -- they used to play for days on end. Now she's so good at it she plays solitaire. For hours all you will hear from her is her rolling those dice. Just give her a flat surface where she can set it all up and you can pretty much forget her for the entire day. Except for meals, of course."

Charmaine actually smiles as she says all this, with Pip still standing right beside her.

Charmaine consults her watch and catches her breath. "Gotta go," she says urgently. She bends down and gives Pip a perfunctory peck on the cheek, does a finger wave at me and says, "Thanks – see you around nine."

Pip and I both go to the door to see her off, both of us, I think, terrified of being left alone with each other. Charmaine half-sprints down the hall toward the elevator bank. I can't help but admire her: her long brown hair is as perfect as it was at Ulrich's christening nearly thirteen years before. Her form-hugging skirt accentuates a lovely figure and her lean bare legs. A thought comes to me that had not registered when I was facing her: her silk blouse is far too sheer for any serious workplace I remember. *A software gaming company*, she had said the other day on the phone. I don't know anything about the modern workaday world but I suspect that digital whiz-kid nerds don't waste much time admiring pencil skirts and bare legs.

I hear Charmaine's elevator door close. I close my door on her, wishing for her some sort of peace and satisfaction during her day.

I smile down at Pip who smiles up wanly at me. I notice there is less life in her eyes now than there was just the minute before. I realize that the glistening brightness in her eyes is really a glazing of illness. Her nose runs. She licks at the effluent. She will not use a hand to wipe her nose because she stills hugs her game box with those skinny desperate arms. I feel her forehead. Pip's eyes close immediately. A look of sensual surrender comes over her little exhausted face, as if she has hungered all her life for someone to touch her tenderly. She's burning up.

"How long have you felt badly?" I ask.

"I didn't feel so well when I went to bed last night."

"Is your throat sore?"

"A little."

"Your mom didn't give you anything for that?"

"I didn't tell her anything. She's got her own problems."

"Do your ears ache?"

"Yes. My right one really badly."

Really badly. I take a moment to be really impressed.

"Well, I don't think you'll be playing any Axis and Allies today," I say, relieved that I won't have to cringe every time she clacks those dice. "I'm going to heat up some chicken vegetable soup for you. You'll have that, a glass of orange juice, half a Tylenol with a glass of water and off you'll go to bed."

Pip seems to like my take-charge attitude. But she looks at me with those big brown eyes and says, "I don't have any 'jammas."

"You'll get under the covers in your undies."

I think about that. It's only Thursday. The once-weekly maid service won't come until tomorrow afternoon. Today is near the end of my cycle of personal cleanliness and things aren't pretty in my bedroom.

"I'll put fresh sheets and blankets on my bed and turn up the heat."

After I sit her down to her soup and orange juice I go into my bedroom. I struggle with that fitted sheet for all the time that Pip is at the dining room table. By the time I get the sheet on and make the rest of the bed my finger and back muscles feel as though they've done a full day's work in a cotton field. I have to sit down for a minute to gather myself.

"The bed's ready when you are," I say to Pip as I come back into the dining area.

"Okay," she says weakly.

I sit with her as she finishes the last of her soup and juice. I feel her forehead again.

"You're warmer now than when you arrived." I try to keep the worry out of my voice. "I'm going to get the thermometer."

I go to the bathroom and rummage around in the medicine cabinet for the little plastic cup in which I kept the thermometer for decades at Paloma. It isn't there. By the time I find it – in a place I had never placed it before: my travel shaving kit which I have not used in a good ten years – I feel a pressing call of nature. By the time I finish and come back out Pip is in the bed and fast asleep.

She sleeps like a log. I'm relieved. I'm not sure what I would have done if her throat or ears had bothered her enough to keep her awake. I try to recall my parenting days with her mother and her grandmother, but no details return to me except Dottie walking around a child's room with a child in her arms, singing a lullaby – I can't recall whether it's Melissa or

Charmaine she's holding because they both had lots of late-night and early-morning ear aches.

Pip sleeps so heavily, with such a look of relief and contentment on her little face. I look in on her every time I hear the sheets rustle. Finally, on my third look-in, I pull up a chair and just watch her. I feel so powerful. I can't remember the last time that I myself had taken charge of a beloved someone and brought relief and comfort to that someone's life. It had not happened in my years as a father and grandfather to adolescent children. I vaguely recall making something of a difference in the lives of a few of my students but I recall no details. Lord knows I hadn't managed to bring any real comfort to Dottie during the last brutal year of her life.

I finally drink my fill of Pip sleeping. I go and sit at the table in front of my sun window which overlooks the Argyll meditation garden some five stories below. I continue to savor my modest little human victory, listening to Pip snore lightly, planning an extravagant lunch for her that I will have brought up to my room if she's too ill to go down to the dining room. I enjoy the sun's warmth and try to nap sitting upright. There is nothing else I can do without risking Pip's sound sleep. I don't own earphones for my stereo, so I can't listen to my music.

I don't really feel like reading. I go to the kitchen and pour myself a glass of cranberry juice. I settle in at the dining room table to flip through a magazine. Pip's game is there in its box.

Milton Bradley Game Master Series. Axis & Allies. A Game of High Adventure.

I pull the box toward me.

I study the box cover. I shudder, my chest tightens, seizes up. Ancient memories and last night's nightmares flood into me. I intend to shut my eyes but the box top images hold me and fix me to eyes-wide-open attention. A cool hardened German field marshal obviously references Rommel. Yamamoto is there. Patton. Doolittle, I think. Eisenhower. On the side of the box top MacArthur puffs placidly on his corncob pipe as he watches some distant explosion through his sunshades. National flags flutter violently. Tanks clank forth. Battleships blaze away at each other. A Stuka dives on Polish civilians. B-17's lumber on to deliver their death loads. British soldiers rush the barbed wire at El Alamein. A U-boat skims the Atlantic waters in pursuit of a kill.

Lord in Heaven, how in the world does any responsible mother end up having a nine-year-old *girl* addicted to this stuff?

I gingerly open the box. All of the battle pieces are in little sandwich baggies segregated by class – infantrymen, tanks, fighters, bombers, antiaircraft batteries, battleships, submarines, merchant ships, little white pieces which seem to represent factories. An old stop watch is in a smaller blue baggie. I shiver involuntarily at the detail on the pieces, at the infantrymen especially whose faces and postures are rendered in such detail that they seem to have distinct personalities: the German infantrymen advance confidently and arrogantly; the English infantrymen seem tentative and unsure. I can bear to look at the face of an American infantryman for only a few seconds. I see faces there, men I've known, who didn't come back. *Ancient memories. Last night's nightmares.*

I extract all the sandwich bags – I can't help myself -- and a thick rule book. I take out the board and unfold it. It's roughly a three-foot-by-two-foot board, a multi-colored map of the world. The world is divided into the regions, provinces and colonies over which the world's great powers fought World War Two.

I'm quaking now. Every where I look on the map I see shredded skin and splintered bone. It is not the spring of 1942 as the box top says; it is specifically June 6, 1944. Early morning. Against my will, my eyes sweep over the board map and settle on the west coast of France. I shiver. I am cold. I am wet. My hundred pounds of equipment crush my back. I cannot breathe. A canvas sheath makes it hard for me to grasp the mortar tube and my fingers ache. I wretch violently and throw up on my own boots. I pray to a God I'm not sure is listening and I cry for my mother. The ramp of the assault barge drops into the sand and instantly three buddies in the barge's first rank explode into pieces.

Oh, God, please, God! Mama! Dottie!

I catch my breath. Then I force myself to breathe deeply and rhythmically. I try to void my brain of all conscious thought before the names come, but they come anyway. One hundred eighty-four of them. Mike O'Connor. Sid Tonelli. Frank Zuckerberg. Hal Watkins. Terry Giminksi. Bill Kranitz. Jim Cavalho. Frank Reynolds. Iggy Levtochenko. Wes Hopkins. Robert Suarez. John Setterstrom. Hal Rosenbaum. Tony Passolino. Howard Metcalf. Benny Martino. Will Jenkins. Mike Streicher. Al Collins. Jim Richmond. Ozzie McCluskey. Lemuel Halberstam. John Runyon. John Miles. Those twenty-four in just that very first minute on the beach. I weep a little. That makes the breathing easier but I grow nauseous and light-headed.

I start the recitation of names all over again, listing them in the chronological order of their loss to me. From the moment that the barge ramp drops to the moment that Den-Den Perkins dies of a drug overdose while we are waiting in Antwerp for a ship to take us home,

I call out the names. For a lot of them I even know their middle initials. I recite slowly, reverently, conjuring up their faces as they looked in basic training when we were fresh and fearless and were going to save the world. I make a game of recalling the best joke I heard from each of them. I remember their mothers' names, the names of a few of their sweethearts. I take all the time that it takes the sun to arc across my sun window, throwing light and warmth in my direction as I sit at the dining room table shivering in my private darkness. The day's rising warmth is my only tether to present-time consciousness. I stay in the past until Pip wakes up in early afternoon. She calls out a name as if startled. *Becky* or *Checky* I think. She whimpers, emits an animal-like grunt. Sheets rustle violently. She seems to come fully alert and shouts out, "I'm hungry!"

We have missed lunch in the Argyll dining room. I make ham and cheese sandwiches in my toaster oven and heat up more soup. I slice up some tomatoes and avocadoes. I take out a pint of vanilla bean ice cream to let it soften. Pip gobbles down everything, all the while looking at me as if I'm some sort of magician-god.

"You're a great cook," Pip murmurs.

I laugh. "This is hardly cooking."

"It's great."

"Is your mom a good cook?" I venture cautiously.

Pip shrugs. "She does her best."

"What did you eat this morning?"

"I didn't. Didn't feel well enough to eat."

"What about last night?"

"Some soup. Not as good as this though. That's all I felt like. You aren't eating?"

"Not much of an appetite."

"Why not?" she asks, frowning. There is adult-like concern in her voice and for a moment I feel cared for.

"I just don't eat much these days. You don't eat much when you get my age."

"But you've got all of this food on hand."

You've got all of this food. Not: *You got all this food.* And it's *on hand*.

"When you get my age," I say, "oat meal and a boiled egg is just fine for breakfast, and a sandwich and a bowl of soup are just fine for lunch. I usually eat a big dinner though. Dinners here are really good."

I put a hand up to her forehead: she is much cooler.

"Maybe you and I will eat downstairs tonight if you feel up to it."

"Yeah," she says in a flat tone. "How old are you?"

"Oh, at last count, eighty-three."

"Wow."

"Impressed?"

"Yeah," she says sincerely. "I've never *met* anyone who is really that old… I mean congratulations on lasting so long. It's a tough world out there."

I'm too stunned to speak. What nine-year-old talks like that?

"How's your young world spinning these days?" I ask cautiously.

"It's okay," she murmurs, her frank eyes looking away from me for the first time and turning down into her soup bowl. "May I set up Axis and Allies now, please?"

May I?

"Now?" I say. "The rule book says it can take up to six hours to complete a game. I imagine it takes much longer when you're playing solitaire."

"But I can continue tomorrow if you leave it up."

"You won't be here tomorrow. You won't be back until next Thursday."

Pip frowns in confusion, the first genuine little girl expression I have seen from her. "Mom says I will be here every week day."

As I look into those intense and intelligent eyes, I know that she has heard her mother correctly. Charmaine has wrung a modest commitment from me and has told Pip to expect something quite different. Despite my decade's absence from Charmaine's life, I feel so confident in thinking that all this is so typical of her, that nothing essential in her has changed.

"Let me make this clear right now so that there will be no misunderstanding," I say sternly, actually talking to the absent Charmaine, "you'll be with me here only on Thursdays, okay? Thursdays only."

My misplaced anger doesn't phase Pip in the least. She nods solemnly and says:

"Then you've got to play with me. We can finish a game today if you play. Even with me teaching you the rules as we go along, we can have a really good game."

"No, thanks," I say quickly.

"Come on. Mom says you were a math teacher. Math and English, right? There's a lot of math in the game. You'll enjoy it."

"No, I won't," I say bluntly.

"Why not?" she says frowning.

"Don't want to talk about it."

I had never talked about it. Not even to my son Brad when he had begun to gravitate toward military history in his adolescent years, not even when he announced in his junior year in high school that he was interested in West Point and a military career and wanted my opinion.

"Do you like chess?" I say a little desperately. "We've got some nice chess and checker tables downstairs in our community room."

A blank calm settles over Pip's face, as if she is armoring herself. She spoons into her bowl for more soup but the bowl is empty. Disappointment rolls in a slow wave over the blankness in her face.

"We have more," I say as I rise.

"No, thank you."

As I look at her I mull over the possibility that she is adopted and has learned her life's manners in some household other than Charmaine's. A memory comes out of nowhere: Dottie and me in bed, her nestling up in the crook of my arm and saying maybe we should consider adoption if we don't get pregnant in another year or so. No, I say. We'll be all right.

"Okay," I hear myself say to Pip. "One game. But I've got to be the Allies, the American side. I can't be the Germans."

"You got it!" Pip cries out, her eyes blazing.

Axis and Allies

We take the game box to the table in front of my sun window. Pip opens the board on the table and immediately clicks on the stop watch without taking it out of its baggie. She sets everything up: my American-British Commonwealth-Russian side as well as her German-Japanese Axis side. She knows all the initial placements by heart: x number of tanks, y number of infantry and z number of fighters in Ukraine; x number of infantry, y number of fighters and bombers and z number of transports in Eastern United States. There are over a hundred fifty pieces to be placed in about sixty regions and provinces at the game's beginning. She moves all the pieces into place as readily as an adult would set up a checkers board.

"An infantry unit only destroys a unit it's attacking if it rolls a one," she says, her little hands a whirlwind of dexterous activity. "But if an infantry unit is defending itself against an attack, then it destroys the attacker if it rolls a one or a two." She pauses and fixes me with her big eyes, assessing whether I'm following her. "Attacking fighters destroy their targets if they roll a one, two or three; defending fighters score hits if they roll a one, two, three or four. Bombers successfully attack on die rolls one through four. However, a bomber's defensive power is an entirely different matter…"

On she goes at a measured pace, in a professorial tone. Somehow I manage to absorb the rules without really being interested in them – my attentive powers are entirely concentrated on drinking in her sweet little face and her impeccable grammar and diction.

"And, despite their offensive firepower, tanks can only defend themselves with die rolls of one and two. This is because they are such clumsy lumbering targets…"

Lumbering.

"A tank can't even defend itself well against a courageous infantryman who can slip in behind it and throw a grenade or a Molotov cocktail down on a tank's hot exhaust grill – exhaust grills can never be armor plated. That's how the Soviets chewed up all those panzers at Stalingrad."

My head throbs. I think of Frank Lamb squatting futilely in front of that Tiger tank near Saint Lo with his bazooka. I cast about desperately for a way to back out of my commitment to play. Dottie reminds me that a responsible adult never, ever, breaks a commitment made to a child.

Set-up time: thirty minutes, the rule book advises. Pip has done it in twelve. Well, actually…

"Twelve minutes ten seconds," Pip says as she studies the stopwatch she has just clicked off. She purses her lips in tentative satisfaction. "Ulrich's personal best is nine forty-three. But he didn't have to teach you things as he was setting up."

"I'm sorry to be such a burden," I laugh.

She smiles, embarrassed in a very adult way by her little flash of rudeness. I catch my breath. She is such a beautiful creature when she smiles. But there is great sadness in her. I venture forth: "Ulrich sounds like he's a very good teacher."

"The best," she says matter-of-factly as she puts the stopwatch aside. "Now," she announces dramatically, "we begin." Her hand sweeps slowly over the board. "It's the spring of 1942, great granddad. The Soviets are reeling from the German invasion of the summer of 1941.

The Germans are regrouping for another summer campaign but their war economy is under great strain. The British are already exhausted and losing all over Asia, in North Africa and in the battle for the North Atlantic. America hasn't really been much help up until now, but its awesome industrial strength is about to kick in."

"I feel overwhelmed already," I say, feeling overwhelmed already.

"It's a lot to process, I know," she says soothingly. "I'll give you helpful hints along the way. Here's the first: I'm trying my best to knock the Soviets out of the war in four turns. If I succeed, things unravel for you very quickly. You have got to keep the Soviets in the war. You've got to – that's the whole key, great granddad. Use America's industrial strength to build fighters and bombers as fast as you can; and get them to England as fast as you can so that you force Germany to split its war production between tanks to attack the USSR and fighters to defend its industrial base against British-American bombing attacks. That way, Germany can't concentrate on building all the tanks it needs to drive the Soviets out of the war."

I hear all of it somehow, but I'm still stuck on *Soviets*. Does she really understand the distinction between Soviets and Russians?

"What grade are you in?" I ask.

"Fourth."

"Do they teach history in fourth grade these days?"

"Not much."

"How in the world do you know so much?"

She shrugs. "Ulrich. I learn everything from him. He's only twelve but he just knows everything. He skipped two grades. Did you know that?"

"No, I didn't," I say humbly.

"Yeah, third and fifth," she says nodding like a proud parent. "Officially, he's in tenth grade now, but he's already doing trig and basic calculus with special tutors when mom can afford them. Ordinary teachers can't teach him enough."

She says it with fierce pride but in slow deliberate pace, never pausing in her unnecessary straightening of pieces on the board, in her fastidious straightening of the unit-storage trays for the five combatant countries.

"The Soviet Union moves first. That's you. I'll tell you now, my first move as Germany will be to batter Karelia. Then I go after the Caucasus. If I succeed, you lose six industrial production points right off the top. So, you've got to shore up Karelia and the Caucasus as much as you…"

She isn't a little girl now. Her pointing finger sweeps over the board like a supreme commander's as he briefs his subordinates, just as Eisenhower is doing on the box top. She gives me a few more tips on being the Soviet commander and advises me on the most effective co-ordination efforts among the three allies.

"Got it?" she says brightly.

"Got it," I say, fighting depression.

"Okay, here we go," she says. "Russia's in the batter's box."

But she directs me closely, practically ordering me in all my moves: use my industrial replacement points to build eight new infantry units; move existing Moscow-region units into Karelia; send my transport ship off to England; concentrate my far east forces in Yakut SSR. All of this takes perhaps five minutes. I don't attack anywhere, so there's no need for me to roll dice.

"Oooo-kay," Pip says with expectant delight, "Deutschland's up." She moves her German pieces with the sure hand of a chess player who has rehearsed this particular gambit time and again. German units seem to fly all over western Europe, eastern Europe and Africa: German submarines slip into the North Sea; a bomber flies off to attack a British battleship in Gibraltar; a tank is shipped to North Africa to re-enforce attacks on British units in Egypt. Then, just as she promised, eight tank, eight infantry and two fighter units from Germany,

Norway, France, Eastern Europe and Ukraine fall upon Soviet forces in Karelia.

"This is what Ulrich calls the all-in gambit," Pip says as she continues moving her pieces into place. "Germany risks everything in the first round of the game. If the dice go my way on sixty percent of the rolls in the first two rounds, I take all of Africa and its rich resources *and* neutralize Russia as a power-player. In round three or four, Germany and Japan together virtually knock Russia out of the war. Then…"

Virtually.

"It didn't happen this way in the real world, thank God," she says, much as an adult would during a casual dinner conversation. "But it could have if Hitler hadn't been so stupid. Ulrich says most historians think that Hitler should have come to some sort of peace agreement with England and France before he attacked the Soviet Union, but Ulrich says he never should have invaded western Europe or bombed England in the first place, not even after provoking them with his invasion of Poland. He just should have built a defensive line along the Rhine and attacked Russia right off. He would have won in the east by 1941 and earned at least a political settlement in the west by 1942. He *really* fucked up. Hitler, I mean."

Her language shocks me. I study her as she continues moving her German pieces into attack position. I keep waiting for her to realize what she has just said, to throw her hands up to her mouth in mortified embarrassment and for abject apology to flood into those big brown eyes.

Finally, cautiously, I say: "Your mother lets you use that sort of language?"

"What? Fuck?" Pip shrugs. "She doesn't like it. But Ulrich uses it and she can't stop him because he gets so wrapped up in the game. Mom's all right with it as long as we limit our language to the game. She says it's actually good practice for us in learning to modify our language to suit different social situations. But she just says that so she can pretend to still have some sort of control over us. That's what Ulrich says anyway."

"Smart guy."

"The smartest," Pip says proudly. "You know how sometimes you see these chess masters playing a game without looking at the board because they've got everything in their heads? Ulrich can do that with Axis and Allies."

"Wow," I say, really impressed. I venture out cautiously: "Does Ulrich always take the Axis side?"

"Yeah. And he always wins too – except this one time that he allowed me do-overs in this really critical sea battle off the Carolines." She points to a group of islands in the Pacific.

"Do-overs?"

"He let me roll the dice again after my first rolls went so badly against me. Ulrich said that we had just too good a game going to ruin it with such improbable outcomes on the dice. I mean, I've got *five* American fighter units attacking his Japanese transports that are loaded with tanks and *not one* of them can roll a one, two or three? Are you kidding me? Ulrich is like: give the girl a freaking break here. So he gave me do-overs and the game just got better and better. I beat him. The only time I did."

"Ulrich sounds like a really good sportsman – and a really good brother."

"He is," Pip nods solemnly. She sighs heavily and purses her lips. These seem to be expressions of satisfaction over what she sees on the board rather than any connections to Ulrich.

She picks up four dice and begins shaking them in her little palm. She looks at me, smiling. "Gotta be honest with you, great granddad. You don't stand much of a chance this first game. But I don't want you to get discouraged. You've got all summer to improve."

"I'm in your hands here," I murmur. The *all summer* weighs on my chest like a millstone.

"We always throw the dice into the box top," Pip says as she places the box top upside down at the end of the table. "We can throw them really hard without them flying all over the place... Okay, here we go. In Karelia, my eight tank units are attacking. These four dice are the first wave of tanks – I like to attack in waves."

"Sounds like an Ulrich tactic," I venture.

"Yeah," she says readily. She stops clacking the dice and opens her palm for both of us to look at them. "You wouldn't think it makes a difference – you'd think these are just a bunch of dumb dice and it doesn't matter how you throw them, but it does. Ulrich says it's all a matter of your own intention and confidence and directing that intention and confidence from your own brain to your dice hand through electro-kinetic energy."

"Can Ulrich really do that?"

"*Boy*, can he," she says emphatically. "A lot of times he needs his infantry to roll ones to get out of a jam? Get this: four of his six infantry will roll ones! Think about it: there is only a one-in-six chance of rolling a one; so you would expect that when you roll six dice at once, only one of them would come up a one. *Two* at most, right? But time after time, Ulrich throws six dice and gets four ones. I'm not kidding. I mean, *time after time* he does it. I'm like: Dude, come on, stop showing off."

I smile into her smile. Without any conscious intention on my part, my hand rises from the table and caresses her little head. Oblivious to my touch, she clacks the dice violently in her fisted hand. My heart freezes: I hear the staccato of German machine guns on the bluffs above the beach.

"Watch your ass!" she screams.

She flings the four dice into the box with such violence that I hear explosions. Troop carriers are ripped apart, broken bodies fly up into the air.

"Three hits out of four!" she cries. "*Three!*"

Her exclamations of satisfaction over the roll outcomes are instantly my buddies yelling for help, for morphine, for someone to just shoot them in the head and put them out of their misery. Pip doesn't notice my pained grimace. She is already retrieving the dice to roll her second wave of tank attacks.

"Watch your ass," she warns again. She clacks the dice violently and throws them down into the box top making more explosions go off in my brain. "Two more hits!" she cries. "Five out of eight for my tanks!"

She continues the process, throwing for two waves of infantry and two fighters that she throws into the battle. The eight infantry get two hits; both fighters get hits.

"Nine hits altogether!" she cries with delight. "Only one of your units is going to survive in Karelia. Everything else is doomed to death. The best you can hope for is that your doomed troops fight with honor and take as many Germans with them as they can."

Doomed troops fight with honor. *You are nine!* I want to scream. I feel deathly old. I'm already exhausted by this game and by her.

"Now your turn to defend," she says handing me the dice. "You've got six infantry, two tanks, two fighters and a submarine. I'll walk you through the battles one by one. Start with your six infantry."

The dice are heavy in my cupped palm. They are hot, they burn me. In my churning brain I feel their edges to be razor sharp. They cut into my flesh.

"Six infantry," I say weakly.

I shake the dice without enthusiasm and drop them into the box. They clunk flatly and are soon still. Pip is stunned.

"Two ones and two twos?" she says, distressed. Four of her eight tank units are now gone.

"Now, my two tanks," I say. I roll two dice.

"Damn, two hits," she says, staring at the one and the two as if they have betrayed her.

"Now my two fighters," I declare as I roll two dice.

"Two hits," she moans.

"And now my submarine."

Will she explode if I roll a hit here? God, don't let it be a one or a two. God, please.

"Hey," I say to take some tension out of the moment, "why does a submarine get to defend itself in a land battle between tanks and infantry units? That's a bit silly."

"No, not at all," she says in a professorial tone. "Karelia is a land mass, sure, but it's got several ports where ships and submarines dock. Fighters strafe and bomb ships in port all the time. Tanks roll up to the docks and blast away at ships at point plank range. So why shouldn't submarines be able to fire their deck guns at attacking units? Sub deck guns can bring down low-flying fighters, they can knock the treads off tanks, they can machine-gun infantrymen running on the docks."

"Ah," is all I can say.

"Now roll," she says impatiently. "A one or two and you've got another hit."

I limply shake one die and drop it into the box.

She looks at the die, stares at me as if I've played a vicious practical joke on her.

"No way," she rumbles.

"Well, way," I say lightly.

She glares at me as if she has caught me cheating. I see this only out of the corner of my eye. I can't bear to look at her, at her or Ulrich.

"Nine hits altogether," she announces bleakly. Her big doe eyes are now slits of suspicion. "You play a lot of craps or something?"

"Never."

"Well, I've never seen anyone roll nine hits on eleven low-probability defenses. Not even Ulrich does that." Her whole body seems to inflate as her eyes bore right through me. "All of my panzers are flaming hulks – my march on Moscow's going to be delayed now for at least two turns."

It's an indictment.

"Well, don't look at me!" I say laughing.

She is not amused. "I'll roll in Gibraltar and Africa now, before we do the death round in Karelia."

She wins handily in Gibraltar and in North Africa.

"Just the one infantry left in South Africa now," she says smugly. "It will be dead in two more turns. Now, back to Karelia. You got lucky in the first round. Now I'm going to burn your ass."

I don't like that at all – don't like the language and especially don't like the arrogance.

She obliterates my one surviving infantry unit in Karelia. I am a little angry. I am doubly angry when I roll a five in my own defense and the unit fails to take a German unit with it.

We battle on for two hours. I get the hang of the game pretty quickly, being a fast learner and having an excellent instructor. I manage to hold the line in the Caucasus and distract her from further attacks there by initiating an Anglo-American bombing campaign against German-occupied France and Germany itself. I compel her Japanese forces to hold back units in the home islands to counter a modest American invasion fleet I keep off Midway Island.

Despite her early flashes of arrogance and poor sportsmanship Pip seems to thrill to the challenge. And *I* thrill immensely to the challenge. Let a smart-mouth nine-year-old make an old fool of me, a teacher and a serious scholar of history? I laugh when my second motive finally percolates up into my consciousness: let *a girl* beat me at a boy's game? I feel younger. I roll the dice with a bit more élan.

"Why are you so happy so suddenly?" Pip asks with an adult's sulking tone.

"Not so suddenly," I say. "Just happy to be doing well." I wink at her. "I don't want to bore you."

"You've played this before," Pip says in accusation.

"Nope. Never seen the game until today."

Pip puffs out her indignation. "Never, huh?"

I distinctly hear in her voice the echo of an older sibling's attempt to intimidate her.

She builds bombers and marshals her forces in France and Norway for an attack on England. It is the lull before the storm. She does not speak. I don't either. I think about how calm I am now as I watch her decide who will die in her next turn as a German commander. I ponder the terror and the agonies of men whose deaths inspired this game. I think again of my losses on Omaha Beach. I think of all that I had not shared with Dottie when I came home from war, the stuff I had kept from her even when I woke her up with my screams, my cries, my violent thrashings of the mattress as I fought to get out of my back pack and jump over the side of the invasion barge before German bullets shredded me.

"Another one, honey?" Dottie would say when I shot bolt upright in bed in the middle of the night. "Oh, God, just tell me, honey. It would help you so much if you just talked to me."

But I wouldn't talk. I cried but I didn't talk. She would cradle me as I cried. After a while she would cry too.

"You should see a psychiatrist at the VA," she would say.

"I'm not crazy!" I would explode at her.

"No, no, I'm not saying that –"

"What are you saying then? You think I'm crazy! I saw things, Dottie! I did things! I've got a right to *screeeam!*"

The volume of my screaming at her, the wildness in my eyes, terrified Dottie. After months of screaming, when I finally realized that she would slip into the bathroom and cry for hours when she thought I had fallen back to sleep, I stopped screaming.

It is now Pip's third turn as the Japanese commander. She

wolfishly eyes weakly defended Alaska. She smiles at vulnerable Australia. But she looks up at me and says, "I'm hungry again. Could we go eat before I do Japan?"

"Of course," I say, relieved. I feel her forehead. That look of warm surrender comes over her again and I just want to take all of her into my arms. "You're still a little warm."

"Just overheated from all that winning," she says grinning.

"Well, I don't want to risk your getting out and about downstairs though. I'll order some food up for us."

"Okay," she murmurs. The brutal warlord has left her completely now. She is little Pip again.

"I want you to have a glass of orange juice and lie down until our dinner comes up."

"Okay."

I'm making up things. I have no reason to order this. I just like my role, I love that look in her eyes when I order her about. If there is such a thing as a clean-old-man-around-a-vulnerable-little-girl, that is what I feel like and I'm addicted to the feeling.

As Pip sips her orange juice, we review the menu sheet which is slipped into every Argyll mailbox at the beginning of each week. She is so excited by her choices: mixed garden salad or shredded cabbage salad; clam chowder, beef barley or minestrone soup; poached salmon, roasted chicken or vegetarian lasagna; cake, pie or ice cream; soda or fruit juices.

She makes her choices very deliberately, savoring every one. I call the kitchen and order. When I hang up, she's looking at me like I'm that magician-god. I finally understand she has never exercised much choice in her world and that she probably has not seen her harried mother exercise much power over her own life. She finishes her orange juice and lies down obediently. I close the curtains in my bedroom and close the door on her. As soon as I do, I feel exhausted and allow a dozen aches and throbs to have their say. I realize that, in addition to having missed my afternoon nap, I've actually stood over that game board for *four* hours. I can't recall the last time I've stood for longer than fifteen minutes.

The doorbell rings. I hear Pip jump up in the bedroom. Mary-Lee, one of the dining room waitresses, comes in with a cart laden with soups, salads, entrees and sweets. We three spread it out on the dining room table. I can't help but fix on how happy and in-control Pip seems as she helps. This is a very special event for her. I pray that it isn't the quantity of food that makes it so.

Pip eats quickly and hungrily but with excellent manners. She chews urgently but thoroughly and silently, with her lips sealed, seeming to savor every mouthful despite her speed.

"Where did you learn your good table manners?" I ask.

After a deliberate swallow she says, "My mom."

"She's done a very fine job."

Pip shrugs. "That's mom," she murmurs with a very adult sarcasm. "She lets us swear like demons over the game board but she's just this little dictator at the dinner table." She mimics her mother with a high-pitched voice: "Don't do this, don't do that, watch your elbow, try to take a little bit of meat and a little bit of vegetable on one forkful, swallow your food before you take a sip, sip don't gulp, wipe your mouth after every sip." Her eyes go bulbously toad-like, as if she's a Vaudeville clown going off on cue. She lifts these tense clawed fingers up to her face like she's going to scratch her eyes out. I nearly spit out my food, I laugh so hard. We laugh together. She has such a sweet girlish laugh – until it winds down and is punctuated by this devilish low-tone that sounds a little dirty. I think *Ulrich* for some reason.

When I again get hold of myself I ask, "Ulrich has good manners too?"

"The best," she says grimacing. "He's so disgusting."

"Disgusting? How?"

"He sucks up to mom with his table manners. He's just this perfect little gentleman with every bite. Hah, you should see how he stuffs his face when mom's not around. Sickening."

The phone rings. I ignore it.

"Aren't you going to get that?" Pip asks.

"No," I say emphatically.

It's my world: Pip and me – and Ulrich. No intrusions.

But shortly after the phone dies away, Pip's smock pocket buzzes obscenely. She pulls out this jet-black cell phone with a hundred buttons and a little television screen on it. She studies the screen.

"It's mom," she says with a glow. She punches a cell phone button. "Hi, mom."

A pang of jealousy stabs me when I see the bright smile on her face.

Charmaine has called to let me know that the work day has gone really well for her. She tells me how she drove like a crazy woman to arrive only ten minutes late that morning, how she solved two critical problems for her boss, how much time it saved the whole office, how everyone appreciated what she had done. I settle in to listen to her prattle on about herself until she suddenly delivers the punch line: she can get off a little early today – she'll be there in half an hour to pick up Pip.

"Don't rush," I say suddenly alarmed. "We're quite settled in here and having a good time."

"No, we'd better get down to the San Mateo Bridge while we can. There's some sort of rock concert tonight at the Shoreline. There'll be a lot of traffic headed south. I'll call you when I'm three minutes away. Can you come down to the car courtyard with Pip so that she can jump right in and we can get on our way?"

"Sure," I say, depressed.

I hang up on Charmaine without a gracious close-out. I'm in such an instant funk. I'm the kid who has been promised a bunch of death-defying rides at the carnival but who is being dragged away after just one ride in the whirling tea cups. What right has Charmaine to truncate my evening with Pip after promising me 'til *eight-thirty or nine*? I can't believe that was only this morning.

I hurry Pip through the rest of her meal. She too seems a little depressed.

"Sad?" I ask.

"Yeah."

"Why?"

"It's a good game we've got going. It's really good. Now we have to break it down."

"No, we don't. I'll keep it up. It will be waiting for you next Thursday."

"Really?" she says, bursting with joy.

She reaches out and covers my hand on the table. She caresses it as she beams at me and continues spooning pie a-la-mode into her mouth. Her manners are suddenly a little sloppy and ice cream oozes through the seam in her thin lips. Her eyes return to her dessert plate but she keeps hold of my hand. I look from our hands to her face and back again, and nowhere else. I feel like I'm the most important human being in the world.

I want Pip to go back to her mother looking just as good as she can look – I want Charmaine to see what a good caretaker I can be. I have Pip take off her smock so that I can run an iron over it. I spot-clean some smudges on the smock (that were there, I think, when I opened the door to her that morning). I re-lace her sneakers so that the laces are even and the bow-ties are nice and symmetrical.

Pip's phone rings. She answers it. "It was mom," she says when she hangs up. "She's just around the corner and will be here in two minutes."

My heart sinks. Pip starts punching buttons on her black phone at a million miles an hour.

"What are you doing?" I ask.

"Just taking down a few notes to myself… about what I want to do in the game next week."

A week!

"That's one fancy phone you've got there."

"Umm. It's a Blackberry – the best."

"It looks complicated."

"It is. I can't do everything that it can do – not yet anyway. Ulrich can though. It's his."

As she punches away I study her face. I look for a hint of grief or a sense of loss. I see none. She finishes punching her buttons and looks up at me grinning.

"Just want you to know this, great granddad: it's okay for you to study the board while I'm gone. You won't be cheating."

"That's good to know. Thank you."

In the elevator on the way down, Pip takes hold of three of my fingers – that's all her little hand can grasp. "It's been a good day, great granddad," she says seriously, as if complimenting me on a chore she was not confident I would manage well when our day began.

"It's been a great day for me, honey," I say. "Where will you be tomorrow?"

Pip shrugs. "Don't know. I don't think mom knows. We might be home alone."

"What?" I say shocked.

"It happens," she says casually. "It's all good. We just don't answer the door to anyone or turn on the stove when mom's gone. And we heat all our food in the microwave. Mom's afraid we'll burn the house down with the stove. We're okay alone."

I choke back any criticism of that arrangement. I grasp Pip's hand now, and tightly. My heart races with anxiety.

The elevator doors open on ground floor. We get out and walk past the reception/security desk.

"Good night!" Pip says brightly to Molly the night receptionist. "Thank you very much for everything!"

"Why, good night, young lady," Molly says, taken aback by Pip's high spirits. "And you're welcome for everything."

"The people here are really nice," Pip whispers loudly to me as we walk out the front door.

Cynical me would normally interpret all that spirited politeness as home-training fulsomeness which as yet lacks the polish of practice and maturity. But Pip squeezes my three fingers extra hard as she speaks and her big eyes glow with gratitude. I want to bend down and kiss her forehead but my back aches.

"Hi, you two!" Charmaine calls from her car when we emerge into the circular car courtyard. "Had a good day?"

"The best!" Pip practically yells. "Great granddad played Axis and Allies with me! All day!"

Charmaine's eyes fix tensely on me. "Really," she says cautiously. "That was very nice of great granddad." She looks a bit balefully at me. "Did she get to finish dinner?"

"She's finished and full. Even brushed her teeth. She can just slide into bed as soon as she gets home."

"Thanks, granddad – really."

There is such sincere gratitude in Charmaine's voice. I think I see moisture in her eyes but I can't be sure. Her eyes were always so preternaturally brilliant.

"Next Thursday?" I say as I buckle Pip into her seat harness.

"Thursday for sure."

What am I saying? I want to say, *No, tomorrow. I want her tomorrow!* But some stupid sort of pride traps all that in my throat and I end up choking it all back.

"I'm really looking forward to it."

I squeeze Pip's shoulder as I say it. She snatches my hand and kisses it. I want to rip her out of that harness and send Charmaine on her way. Charmaine guns the engine and drives off. I stand there watching her tail lights until the car rounds a corner. I continue to look for a while because the now empty space through which the two of them have just moved is so much more warming than the emptiness that waits for me upstairs.

"What a darling girl," Molly says to me when I re-enter the lobby.

"She is," is all I can say.

A Week Without Pip

Thursday evening through the next Thursday morning! My God, how will I survive this? I can't bear to go anywhere near my sun window and have the game board remind me of Pip's absence, of the huge hole in my heart which grows by the hour. I walk around the apartment for a while, flaying myself for not speaking up and volunteering to take Pip for more days. Why didn't I? Why the hell didn't I? Stupid and proud. Just so stupid and so proud.

But that's not it. I know the truth. I allow it to percolate up into my consciousness. For forty years now, I have kept the pain of it in a dark hole covered by layers of disciplined denial. The truth is: I don't want to risk being rejected again by Charmaine. I recall the dynamics of our relationship: the times when I would make the simplest requests of her and she'd go out of her way to do just the opposite in bold-faced spades. Stop picking your nose; pick up after yourself; don't slurp your drink; keep your dress down; watch your temper; get your homework done; study for that math quiz; don't drink; then don't drink around boys; at least, don't get drunk around boys; stay away from that boy; don't drink at parties with older boys; be in by ten; all right, be in by twelve; call us if you're going to be *that* late. With every command, request or supplication came a brutal rejection. That's why I didn't ask. I didn't want to risk losing the one day a week I now had with Pip. As long as Charmaine thought that I was being inconvenienced by taking care of Pip, I was safe. If I shared my need for Pip…

I was sure that Charmaine was still capable of that meanness. Every little bit of her self-absorption was still there, the narcissism, the bitterness. She still, in a way, ignored Dottie as she generally had. Why wouldn't she still be that mean with me? I ask myself that question one more time, then push the whole mess of that history back into its dark hole.

Everywhere there are reminders of my Pip-privation: the game board on the sun window table, the big chunk of leftover pie on the dining room table, the empty soup bowl in the kitchen sink, her rumpled sheets in the bedroom, the smear of her toothpaste in the bathroom sink. I walk from room to room wallowing in my desperation and trying to fight it at the same time.

When I finally allow the day's exhaustion to overtake me, I take a long shower and get ready for bed. Only I stare down at the sheets, Pip's sheets. I can't sleep on them. I leave them undisturbed for the same reason that I had left Dottie's side of the bed undisturbed on Paloma Street: the evidence of her presence is a promise that she will return soon. Pip, I mean. I try to laugh off the sentiment as scary weirdness, as old-man eccentricity perhaps laced with a little dementia, but I can't laugh it off. Just the opposite: I sit gingerly on the edge of the bed and weep.

Eventually I retreat to the living room and make the sofa bed. I sleep fitfully, without dreaming. I get up and take my usual dawn patrol walk around Japantown. When I return to the Argyll, I pick over breakfast and go back up to my apartment. The maid is there and I tell her that whatever she does she is *not* to disturb the sun window table. As an afterthought, I tell her not to change the bed linen as well. I just changed it the day before, I say.

After the maid leaves, I settle into my easy chair and listen to Brahms for the rest of the morning. At noon, I go down to lunch, eat indifferently, come back up and get right back into my sofa bed. When my bones become bed-weary in late afternoon I get up and sit in my easy chair in my pajamas, listening to Chopin ballads and nocturnes, hoping that the music will anesthetize me. When that fails, I eat ice cream by the bowls (an old addiction which I had not indulged since my last days of worrying over the adolescent Charmaine). I don't go down for Friday dinner. I stay in my apartment and eat ham and cheese sandwiches with Progresso soup and avocado wedges. I listen to more music. I try a little television. I flip through old photo albums of the early years of my marriage. When that becomes too depressing, I go to bed early and toss-and-turn through most of the night. When I sleep, I do not dream.

By Saturday afternoon I am desperate. I call Charmaine and tell her that I am willing to take Pip for the whole week, starting Monday morning.

"Oh, granddad, that's great, but Mondays are Pip's appointments with a child psychiatrist out here. After that, a neighbor picks her up and keeps her until I get home. And I've already made pretty good arrangements with my neighbor to take Pip on Tuesday and Wednesday."

"I hope this neighbor is a female neighbor."

"Yes," she says laughing. "A trusted friend. She's got to be home all next week tending to a very ill child. So I'm covered."

"Well, maybe that's not the best for Pip," I say desperately. "It's not such a good idea to have Pip around a sick child."

"Actually the sick child is an infant, granddad. Pip's not at risk. My neighbor is looking forward to having Pip keep her other daughter company all day. They're about the same age. And it's just easier to have Pip near home than have to drive across town to get to your place twice in a day. I get to BART in and out. That's so much easier than the long drive. But I'll see you Thursday. Pip can't wait. You're all she talks about. See you Thursday, okay?"

"Okay," I mumble, feeling thoroughly defeated.

"Good night – thank you." She clicks off.

My loneliness is crushing. I actually feel my heart to be under intolerable pressure, like it's in a vice that is tightening with every beat of my heart. I stand there looking at the dead phone in my hand, listening to the dial tone mock me for my desperation to have again a little girl at whom I had all but sneered when her mother had begged me to take her in. I can't stand my apartment without Pip's presence. I get out – I go back down and sit in the community room. No one is in there but just the thought that others had been there in the hours before makes do as a substitute for companionship. I go to the wall console, punch the "classical" selection and turn on the music to a whisper volume. A Chopin nocturne lilts through the ceiling speakers. I settle into the room's most comfortable easy chair and resign myself to staying there the rest of the evening. I am there about forty minutes when Mary comes walking in with her decrepit German boyfriend. They stop abruptly when they see me, seemingly surprised and displeased that they do not have the whole place to themselves.

"Hello, Mortie," Mary says solemnly.
"Hello, Mary."
"Let's sit over there anyway," she says quietly to her boyfriend.

They continue on toward the far corner where the grand piano and a few sheet music tripods stand. The boyfriend keeps his uncomfortable eyes on me for all the time it takes them to cross the room. I stare right back at him. *Asshole,* I think with some intensity – for a moment not sure whether I'm aiming that at him or at her.

Anyway?

They settle in, across from the other, at a coffee table in front of the piano. They seem content not to speak.

This is all I need, I think self-pityingly. Four more days without Pip and my only friend in the world parading her death-warmed-over boyfriend in front of my face.

Axis and Allies, Round Two

I rise early on Thursday morning. I groom myself like I'm preparing for parade inspection. I pull out all the makings of a good light breakfast and leave my front door open. I set the oven alarm clock for five-twenty that evening. At seven-thirty, Olga calls to inform me that they are here. They come up. Pip looks fresh and expectant; Charmaine already looks a bit tired.

"We're trying a little experiment today," Charmaine says. "We took BART to Civic Center and took a cab here. Tonight, could you cab her to Civic Center and meet me there?"

"Sure," I say. "But how will you get to work from here, and from work to BART this evening?"

"Cab," she says, flinching a little. "Like I said: an experiment."

"That's expensive," I say. "God, it's got to be twenty dollars in the morning traffic." I reach into my candy jar on the entrance table and pull out two twenties. "Here."

"Stop it," Charmaine says emphatically.

"Charmaine, take it."

Tentatively she does, looking at me warily as she folds it. "Thanks." She throws an embarrassed look in Pip's direction. "I brought several of her books," Charmaine says a little loudly. "Just in case she gets tired of playing Axis and Allies. Although I doubt that. It's all she's talked about for the past seven days." She looks at me puzzled, trying to figure out something but reluctant to ask directly for an answer to her question.

"Work as late as you need to," I say. "I'm sure we'll find more than enough to do."

"Okay," Charmaine says. She looks at her watch, throws an air kiss toward Pip and heads for the door.

"Bye, mom," Pip chirps, already hovering over the game board. "Have a great day."

"You too, baby-doll," Charmaine says without conviction.

I watch Charmaine retreat down the hall. Her shoulders are already hunched and her gait a little uneven. *My mom taught me my manners* comes suddenly to mind. I say a silent prayer for Charmaine, for her stamina and her morale.

"Hope you've been studying up," Pip says as I close the door on the back of Charmaine.

"Nope. Haven't even looked at the board."

"You've got to be kidding me."

I lie: "I thought that would be unfair to you since you don't get to see it for a week."

"Oh, I had my Blackberry notes," she says chortling. "And I memorized the board before I left."

"You didn't."

"I did." She turns her back to the board and looks out my sun window. "At Midway, the Americans have two aircraft carriers, three fighters, two transports, two tanks…" She streams on reciting troop dispositions in three or four other regions.

"All right, all right," I say annoyed. "Stop showing off. Your move with Japan."

We get right down to it. A half-hour passes before I realize that I've forgotten all about the marvelous breakfast I was going to make for her. We fight for hours, stop around noon to have some eggs and ham and jellied toast and hot chocolate, and then fight on. It's touch-and-go all over the world. The Japanese nearly succeed in getting a beachhead in Alaska; I beat them back. My Anglo-Americans are able to land in and hold on to France for a turn, but the Germans drive them back into the sea. A concerted German-Japanese attack threatens my teetering Soviets but some incredibly bad-luck dice-rolling on Pip's part saves my ass there. She looks at me, at first simmering, then with this soft open supplicant's face. I know what she's thinking: *do-overs*. She doesn't want to ask; she wants me to offer. She gets nothing from me.

"Life is tough," I say smugly. "War is worse."

At five-twenty my oven alarm goes off.

"What's that for?" Pip asks.

"To remind us to go down and have a really good dinner. Feel up to it?"

"Sure!"

I look at her dress, those socks, that hair – I'm sure it's the outfit from last week! Suddenly I care that my Argyll neighbors will see me entering the dining room with a ragamuffin whom I have to introduce as my great grand daughter. I think for some reason about the evening elegance of Mary Givens and her friends. I try to run a comb through Pip's hair. Not a single strand submits to my will that it lie down and look civilized. Pip looks at me as I comb. That look of surrender comes over her face again. She obviously interprets my silly vanity as a gesture of love. My heart wants to break.

Going down in the elevator Pip stares up frankly at me.

"You think about your time in the war when you roll the dice," she says. It's a statement, not a question.

"Yes," I say, more unsettled by the adult intent behind that little voice.

"Mom was really surprised when I told her you played Axis and Allies with me. She said I shouldn't bother you with it."

"Why did she say all that?"

"She says you saw things in the war. Horrible things. She says when she was a girl in your house, you used to wake up in the night screaming something awful. She remembers hearing you right through her bedroom wall at night. Great grandma Dottie tried to calm you down, mom says, but it never worked."

"She spoke of great grandma Dottie?"

"Sure."

"Recently?"

"All the time. She loves great grandma Dottie a lot. Mom was very sad for a long time when she died."

I catch my breath.

"How did she know when great grandma Dottie died?"

"Don't know," Pip shrugs. During my stunned silence over this new revelation Pip takes hold of three of my fingers and squeezes gently. "I'm sorry. I shouldn't make you play."

"You didn't make me play today. I wanted to today."

"You wanted to for me. I should have said no for you today. Like you said yes for me last week. I was selfish. We can fold it all up when we come back from dinner."

"It's all right."

"Not if it makes you remember things."

"I remember them anyway, honey."

She squeezes my fingers a little harder in sympathy.

"I know about war," she says ever so quietly. "I've seen pictures. Ulrich shows me lots of pictures. I saw Tarawa and Okinawa and Nanking. I saw the death camps and the frozen dead at Malmedy." She has pronounced *Malmedy* like a French girl.

"Where did he get those pictures?"

"The internet. YouTube, Yahoo Images, Google Images."

I have no idea what she's talking about.

"Well, pictures can't tell you what death is really like."

"I know real death. I've seen it."

"Where, honey?"

"Ulrich. I saw Ulrich."

Her tender grip on my fingers tightens even more. My finger joints actually begin to ache under her pressure.

"I'm so sorry, honey."

I need to know if she actually saw him die or saw him in his coffin, but I'm not sure that I can get there without wounding her. The elevator doors open to a trio of neighbors.

"Hi!" Cu Raley exclaims, her eyes already fixed on Pip. "And who's this sweet little thing we have visiting us tonight?"

Before I can get a word out Pip says, "I'm Amani Carpenter. I'm nine years old and I'm Mr. Willbanks' great granddaughter visiting from Hayward. I'm going to be here on Thursdays until the end of summer."

Cu and the others just stare wide-eyed at Pip.

"And she is extremely shy," I say drolly.

We all laugh.

"'Armani' did you say your name is?" Cu's hard-of-hearing husband asks.

"No, sir, A-man-i. That's Swahili for 'peaceful.'"

"Oh, my," Cu says, not certain whether she should be impressed or sympathetic. "Do you speak Swahili yourself?"

"Not yet," Pip says brightly. "Someday. I'm sorry: I don't know your names."

"Well, I am Catherine Raley," Cu says formally, her eyes fluttering with embarrassment. "This is my husband Tom and our friend Bernie."

The two men nod. "Hello," they say, almost in unison.

"I'm very pleased to meet you all," Pip says, her adult-like poise bordering on impertinence. "You all are dressed so nicely."

"We are going to the opera tonight," Bernie says. "Do you like opera?"

"I just *love* the opera music that I have heard, but I've never seen a real opera," Pip says. "Maybe someday with my great granddad."

The elevator doors open. Cu's party stands closest to the door and people are waiting to get on. But Cu and the men just stand there staring down at Pip like she's some never-before-seen species of mammal.

"Well, here we are," Pip says smiling.

As the men file off the elevator, Cu turns to me and declares solemnly, "You've got one little pistol there, Mort."

"Don't I know it," I say proudly.

The Salad Bar

We enter the dining room at precisely 5:30. We are the evening's first diners. I steer us to a table for four on the periphery of the main dining salon. Pip's appearance is still somewhat on my mind.

"You start by going to the salad bar over there and making as big a salad as you want," I tell Pip. "They've got everything: three types of lettuce; three types of olives; three types of tomatoes; six types of salad dressing; avocados; string beans and green peas; artichokes; hearts of palm; pine nuts; bacon bits…"

"Anything I want?" Pip says, stunned and still skeptical.

"Anything. By the time you get back the waitress will be here with our menus for us to order soups, entrees and desserts. But I can tell you now you'll want to save room for dessert."

"Come with me," she says nervously.

"Go on." My knees ache from standing over the *Axis and Allies* board. "I'm not wasting room on salad tonight. Tonight is rack of lamb and bread pudding."

"Uhmmm, yummie," Pip says, her eyes blazing.

I watch her with great satisfaction as she heads off for the salad bar. She circles the bar marveling at the selections. I once again sense that she has no control over any part of her life and is enjoying this little experience immensely.

Mary Givens enters the dining room from the far community room door. She looks fabulous. She's got on a knitted skirt suit that seems to cling discreetly to every contour of her body. I recognize the brand even from across the room. It's a St. John. Dottie had two of them and saved them for very special occasions. It's gorgeous on her, just gorgeous. And those heels. Maybe she's in her fifties, I think.

Mary goes right to the salad bar. Instantly she's involved with Pip, curious and friendly. I can't hear a word between them but I can tell that Mary is treating Pip like an adult fully deserving of serious adult-level social attention. Pip points in my direction; Mary looks at me and smiles. From the movements of their lips I surmise that Pip is contributing at least half of the conversational freight. Mary laughs heartily at something Pip says and puts an intimate hand on Pip's shoulder.

It takes them forever to make their salads. They seem to talk lettuce leaves and dressings as they circle the bar several times. When they finally finish, Mary walks Pip back to our table.

"Evening, Mortie."

"Evening, Mary."

"Mortie, you've got the most charming, beautiful and brilliant great granddaughter. How do you rate such a fine young woman in your life?"

"A chain of good fortune stretching over several generations," I manage without stuttering.

Pip just beams.

"Well, she's a treasure. I'd like to join you two for dinner if I might."

"Sure. We'd like that, wouldn't we, Pip?

"Yes, very much!"

From the time Mary and Pip sit down, it's essentially a bilateral conversation between the two of them. I don't mind: I get a chance to savor Mary's face and voice without processing a lot of words. They move from Pip's school experience this past school year to Pip's hobbies to Pip's clothing style.

I break in here and say, "I hope, over the summer, to have some influence over that clothing style."

Pip looks down into her salad plate. Mary looks at me for a moment like I've said something incredibly stupid.

Mary says, "A girl who dresses like Pip knows her own mind, right, Pip?"

"Yes," Pip says emphatically, shooting darts at me with those big eyes.

"A girl who knows her own mind grows up to be a woman who knows her own mind," Mary continues. "Not enough of those in the world."

Mary winks at Pip. Pip grins, this huge glorious ear-to-ear grin.

"Hey," Mary says in sudden revelation, "have you heard of Vivienne Westwood?"

Pip shakes her head.

"She's a British fashion designer. A brilliant one. You either love her or you hate her and people with imagination love her. There's an exhibit of her work at the de Young." Mary looks at me. "Maybe we can talk your great granddad into escorting us to the museum tomorrow."

"I won't be here tomorrow," Pip says, deflating in great disappointment. "I'm here only on Thursdays."

"Oh," Mary says, almost as disappointed. "Well, next week then." She suddenly brightens with revelation. "*Or* maybe we just jump in a cab right after dinner and go there this evening."

"Today, you mean?" Pip says inflating again.

"Why not?" Mary says, but looking at me. "The museum closes at 8:45 tonight. Tonight is an extended-hours preview for members only."

"We're not members though," I say.

Mary rolls her eyes. "Then you'll become a member tonight, all right? Anyway, I'm a member. And a docent with contacts."

"Pip's mother will be here in three hours or so," I say.

"Well if we eat with intention, we've got twenty minutes to get there, twenty minutes to get back and as much as two hours in between at the museum."

Pip looks at me afraid to be hopeful, ready for disappointment.

"That sounds pretty good to me," I say almost evenly. My heart pounds with the thought of spending an evening with Mary. I envision us finishing with the museum and my suggesting we go somewhere where Mary and I have wine and Pip has a Shirley Temple. What the hell am I thinking? I've never touched wine, except when we liberated Paris, but I know that Mary likes it.

My heart also pounds with the possibility that I can distract Pip from channeling Ulrich for the rest of our evening together upstairs. "I'll just go upstairs -- make a call to Charmaine, Pip's mother."

"Don't have to, great granddad," Pip says whipping out her Blackberry. "You didn't bring your cell phone down?"

"I don't have one," I grumble, eyeing the instant amusement in Mary's face.

Pip punches buttons with a whirl of fingers. "Mom's number is up on the screen. Just push the green phone symbol and you'll hear her phone ringing." She holds it out to me. I'm flabbergasted by the complexity of the thing.

"I'll step out anyway," I say. "Want to talk over a few things you shouldn't hear."

I go all the way outside. I push the green phone symbol.

"Pip?' Charmaine's worried voice soon responds. "Is everything all right, hon?"

"It's me, Charmaine. I'm calling to get your ok to keep Pip for the night. We're having a great time and we might go to a museum exhibit tonight."

"Is she really feeling up to all that?" Charmaine asks cautiously.

"She's just fine. She's some little trooper."

"How's her appetite?"

"Like a bull moose," I say laughing. "I'm really fattening her up."

Charmaine laughs. "That's sweet, granddad. To be truthful, I've been asked to work after hours tonight. I was just sitting here trying to work up my courage to face one of you: either my boss to tell him 'no' or you to ask you to keep Pip until midnight. Thanks, granddad. God, this helps so much." She sighs. It's a sigh of exhaustion rather than relief. "Give my love to Pip. I'll call her tomorrow morning."

"Will do," I say.

"Thanks." She clicks off.

Mary and Pip make quite a couple in the museum. They are the most conspicuously dressed people there: Mary, elegant in her St. John and sexy high heels, makes many heads turn, particularly male ones; Pip, in her bright ragamuffin outfit, seems a walking breathing mannequin who is highlighting the very styles on display. I trail behind them, savoring Mary's back. They talk patterns and colors and contours and hemlines as they walk about. Mary does most of the talking but I can tell from a distance that Mary is stimulated by Pip's perceptive questions. At one point Pip takes Mary's hand and squeezes it, I think not even aware of what she's doing, not aware of her need. With no apparent sense of surprise, Mary just accepts her hand and encloses it like

Pip is her granddaughter. From that point on, it's just the two of them as far as they are concerned. I don't mind. I'm actually glad for the off-time from Pip. Her world war has gutted me emotionally – I realize that now -- and the big dinner, so much larger than I usually eat, has numbed me.

It takes a little over an hour for us to make it through the entire exhibit. We are on the verge of exiting, of passing the sign that reads, *No re-entry into the exhibit past this point.* Both Pip and Mary stare at the sign with regret. They look at each other. I swear I can just about see undulating waves flowing between their eyeballs. Without exchanging a word, they take each other's hand, turn around and start back through the exhibit. They look at everything again, as if seeing it for the first time. Their conversational exchanges are as animated during this second round they were in the first. I just marvel at the sight of them. I think of Dottie in her sixties, straining with such great love to carry on a relaxed conversation with Charmaine that lasts longer than six sentences. In that moment, my heart both swells for Pip and breaks for Charmaine and Dottie. I can't help but think that I could somehow have smoothed the path for Charmaine and Dottie the way I have tonight for Mary and Pip. As I follow the two of them back through the exhibit I start asking myself: where was I during those years, where was my head?

After two hours, it's nearly closing time. Guards start getting restless.

"Not even time for a light snack?" Pip says plaintively.

"You're hungry again?" I say. "After that huge dinner you had?"

"Hush up," Mary says. "Don't ever make a lady feel guilty about her appetite – for anything."

I hush up, feeling for an instant that the *for anything* contains a deeper message for me rather than emphatic encouragement for Pip. I quickly convince myself otherwise. *You're eighty-three, simpleton. Wake up and calm down.*

At Mary's suggestion, we pile into a cab outside the closed museum and head for her favorite late-night taco place in the Mission. Pip has three tacos and a Jarritos soda! Mary is right behind her with two tacos and half of the beer she shares with me. "Ther-ve-tha," she keeps calling it. Her perfect pronunciation of Spanish food terms soon attracts the attention of three young Hispanic males sitting at a table near us. After smiling through their very frank looks at her, she engages them in a bit of Spanish conversation. The faster and more colloquially they seem to speak to her, the faster and more colloquially she fires back at them. We are all just wowed. Pip looks at Mary like she's an empress-goddess.

"Let's pull our tables together here," Mary says, "so we don't have to shout at each other."

I bridle a bit at that. There was never any prospect of us shouting at one another. Mary just wants to get closer to young men, give them an up-close-and-personal experience with her so that she can savor their wide-eyed wonder.

Mary moderates a bi-lingual six-way conversation with the ease of a UN interpreter. By the time we break up for the evening I know more about life in Mexico and expatriate Mexican life in San Francisco than I can ever remember knowing about my own young adulthood in Indiana. And those young men know more about Indiana small-town life than they ever wanted to know. A bigger surprise to me is that somehow I have eaten my way through a couple of tacos and polished off a second cervesa during the hour and a half that we spend with Mary's new friends.

We close the place. As we walk out, the restaurant staff literally lines up at the door and bows gratefully to Mary. Our young tablemates whistle down a cab for us and bundle us into it with all the attention and deference of a secret service detail taking care of the presidential family.

"Wow, that was intense!" Pip exclaims as she looks back waving at the young men.

"Intense?" I echo in slight confusion.

"You really *like* people, don't you?" Pip says to Mary.

Mary chuckles as she squeezes Pip's hand. "Honey, if you put yourself out and like people just a little bit, they will just love you right back. The world is just full of quaking hearts desperate to be touched."

Mary smiles and keeps her eyes on Pip as she says this. But I am damned sure those words are meant for me, that the smile is meant for me. It's all a sermon. My pride wants me to feel patronized and a bit put off. But I am one of those quaking hearts and I know it.

Pip sits between us holding our hands in her little lap. She is very satisfied with herself and her circumstances. She hums a melody that sounds like it might come from a Disney movie or a children's television program but she is otherwise content to say nothing. I wonder about Mary's silence, I wonder if she is thinking of me as I am thinking of her. I decide that she isn't.

We ride the elevator up, Pip between us, still holding our hands. I can't remember the last time that I felt so satisfied with the very moment in which I am living. *This very moment is so good – this one right now.*

"Life is good." It just bursts out of me.

"Yes, it is," Mary affirms quietly, as if she's been tuned in to my thoughts all the while.

The elevator doors open on the fifth floor.

"Good night," I smile at Mary as I usher Pip out.

"Night, Mortie."

"Good night, Mary," Pip says reverently.

"Nightie night, dear," Mary chuckles.

I'm on the elevator's threshold. Mary pulls me back a step and kisses my ear.

"Happy Memorial Day, Mortie," she says quietly. "Thank you so much for your sacrifices and service."

"Memorial Day?" I say. "That's not until next week."

"Well," she says, "when I'm really grateful, I like to express myself early and often. Thank you."

Again, I feel her lips – this time on my cheek. I say nothing. I move only because Pip's tugging hand prompts me to step out of the elevator with her. The doors close. Mary is gone.

I suddenly feel wrung out by the long day – the longest day of my death watch without a nap. I honestly think I misheard Mary in some way, and that the brush of her lips against my skin was really a strong draught of air rushing up through the seam of the elevator shaft. Now that I'm nearly at my evening's door, I am sure that the more wonderful parts of my day are fragments of an old man's hallucinatory exhaustion. Bonding with a wounded child who wasn't in my life a week ago? Enthusiastically playing a war game – *again* -- after decades of nightly terror? Eating seconds at an Argyll evening meal? Having tacos in an ethnic place in a questionable part of town? Talking like a human being to other human beings whom I had long marginalized as lettuce-picking mannequins in a distant field? A kiss from the most beautiful woman I know? Two kisses! Yes, I think: even for a healthy young man in love with life this has been a mighty fine day.

As I pull out my door key, Pip tugs hard on my fingers and pulls me down to her level. It hurts my back to stoop but I don't want to disappoint her. She has a glow in her eyes. She pulls my face into hers and kisses my cheek. I kiss her back. She glows brighter. I stand up and caress the top of her head as I slip my key into the lock. My old man's room is on the other side of this door, is it not? My old man's life? My old man's nightmares? That much must be real.

Victory in the Caucasus

The next morning I wake up early. I'm disoriented at first because I am on a sofa bed. Why? Then I remember. I ache in every joint but I'm anxious to get at another day with Pip. *But I ache.* I recall that I tried to sort of jump in and jump out of a cab the evening before, to impress Mary with my sprightliness. I lie quietly, marveling that I had not dreamt of that killing beach or of Frank Lamb flying to pieces after his bazooka shot pinged off that Tiger's hull. Somehow I have replaced all that with other dreams, of Pip grasping my hand, of Mary kissing my cheek, of Dottie smiling at me. I listen for Pip's light snoring from the bedroom and hear none. Then I hear her clear her throat meaningfully from the general area of the sun window. I look up over my blanketed feet and see her kneeling in a chair at the table, leaning over the board on her elbows, but looking pointedly at me.

I laugh. "Good morning, general."

"Good morning, great granddad. How did you sleep?" It's a hostess' voice asking how her guest has fared on the guest sofa.

"I slept well, honey," I say, dropping my head back into my pillow. Suddenly, realizing that war waits for me, I wish that I could sleep a few more hours. "How did you sleep?"

"Really well. I've already had some warm milk and buttered toast. I hope that was okay."

"Of course it's okay. This is your little palace. But, you know, if you stay overnight again, *you* will sleep on the sofa and I will sleep in my bed."

"Yeah, makes sense. I made some oat meal and boiled a couple of eggs for you," she says solicitously.

I look up over my feet in surprise. "You did? You know how to do all that?"

She grimaces in very adult fashion. "I'm nearly ten, great granddad."

"So quietly I mean. I didn't hear a thing."

"I learned to make breakfast quietly with Ulrich. So we wouldn't disturb mom in the mornings." She adds ever so suggestively: "I don't mind you eating at the board. Ulrich never lets me do it but I'll let you if you don't hold anything right over the board or over the rule book."

I let my head drop into the pillow again. I suddenly feel a hundred years old in each of my bones. I'm willing to do anything but stand over that board all morning.

"I'm a little tired of oat meal," I say. "Let's go down for breakfast. Get some pancakes, cheese-scrambled eggs and English sausages." None of that really interests me -- I still feel the taco from last night. I hear from Pip a significant silence worthy of her mother.

Finally: "Your world, great granddad. Personally, I'd rather put the time into the game and save up our appetites for a big lunch."

"We can't play all the way to lunch time," I say a little desperately. "I'll certainly need a nap today."

"Well, all right then – we'd better get started."

I get up, collect the day's clothes from the closet and from my bedroom dresser. I go into the bathroom. It takes me a good half hour to negotiate all the morning's necessities. When I come out Pip is practice-throwing dice into the box. I hear distant explosions but I push them back.

"I take the Caucasus this morning," she says. She gives me this steely look, like she's reminding me not to be disappointed in her when she slits my throat. "Some tough times ahead for the Allies. Once the economies of Russian Europe and the Asian mainland are integrated into the Axis war economies it's all over for you."

Ulrich, I think. *How much fun would it have been to have three or four of him in my classes?*

"Let's go," I say.

"No breakfast?"

"No, let's get at it."

She explodes into a huge grin. "Okey dokey," she murmurs.

She starts moving her German units out of Karelia and Ukraine and into the Caucasus. She brings six replacement tanks from Germany. It's eight of her tank units and eight infantry against ten of my infantry units.

"You overcommitted in the east," she says as she picks up the dice. "You needed to keep at least four more infantry in the Caucasus and Moscow regions. Now watch your ass." The fist hand whirls. "Four tanks!"

Two hits. She is pleased.

"My other four tanks!"

One hit. She frowns.

"Armor's faltering," she mutters to herself. "Got to send infantry in as one giant wave." She picks up eight dice. "All eight infantry together. Watch your ass." She clacks the dice violently, shouts, "Bongo!" as she slams them into the box wall.

"Two hits," she says relieved. "Five altogether. Your turn to defend."

I am as repelled and paralyzed by her war heat today as I was the day before. I scoop the dice out of the box and say quietly, "Hand me those extra dice. I'm rolling all ten infantry together." She gives me the extra dice. I shake them all in my two hands without enthusiasm. I think of a thin infantry line I was once a part of in Belgium in December of '44. I drop the dice in the box.

"Damn," Pip says shocked.

I'm surprised myself: I've thrown five hits.

"Statistically, you should have had *two* at most." I don't dare correct her slightly faulty statistical analysis. She's looking at me through those menacing slits. "I'm down to three armor," she says as she removes my five dead infantry and her five dead armor units from the board. She picks up the dice quickly. "Here is the second attack with three armor." She throws three dice into the box without first advising me to watch my ass, without shouting Bongo. Her three tanks score one hit. "And now my eight infantry." She rolls eight dice – none of them a hit. "Damn!" she cries sincerely, almost heartbroken. "Statistically, one of those should have been a one for sure!"

I roll quickly: five dice for my surviving infantry – three hits.

"That's impossible," Pip stutters.

While she is momentarily paralyzed I take her three dead tanks and my one dead infantry off the board.

She is now down to no tanks and eight infantry against my four surviving infantry. Her next round of eight dice yields no hits; my counter-throw yields two hits. It is now her six against my four. She rolls no hits; I roll one. Her five against my four. She rolls one hit and I roll *two*! Her three against my three.

I am into the game now. I know the statistical probabilities are with me and very much against her. She's got to roll ones. I win on ones and twos. I know the Caucasus has a good chance of surviving, the Allies a good chance of winning. I just have to concentrate my will on surviving and transfer that will to the dice. I don't think of France or Belgium in 1944. I think of me, right now, right here, my old man's honor at stake against this little snippet of a girl.

Pip shakes three dice. "Watch your ass now." There is concentration in her tone – resolution – but no arrogant bellicosity.

She rolls: one hit.

"Yes!" she cries.

I pick up the dice. I shake them. I shake them some more. Strangely, I think of Dottie and me in Las Vegas. I remember her aversion to gambling, a deep-seated aversion planted firmly by her six generations of Indiana Baptist heritage. We had gone to Vegas only to see Neil Diamond, Dottie's favorite of all time. Dottie had gotten a little drunk on the complimentary drinks (her Indiana Baptist aversion to drinking not being quite so deep-seated as her aversion to gambling). As we had passed the casino floor on our way to a café, she had impulsively grabbed my hand and pulled me toward the slot machines. She had put in a quarter. Bells and sirens had gone off. Quarters had flooded out of the machine and down on to our feet.

I raise my clenched fist above my ear. The cupped dice are clacking now. Pip looks at me as if I am her mortal enemy. I decide to try something.

"I imagine Ulrich gave you the look you're giving me now when his back was against the wall."

Her expression does not change. "Yeah," she says matter-of-factly. "This is the look. This is the look that wins wars. Watch your ass."

"Hey, I thought the dice-roller got to say that."

"Well, say it then," she says calmly. "Nobody's stopping you."

At the cash-out window, Dottie had immediately pocketed two hundred seventy of the three hundred dollars she had won. But, much to my shock, she had taken the remaining thirty dollars in three ten-dollar chips. She had held them right up under my nose, alcohol glistening in her lively eyes.

"This," she had said solemnly, "is the one and only time in our lives when we will play the roulette wheel. *One and only*. Agreed?"

"Agreed," I had laughed.

Dottie had been cautious at first: one chip on even, win; one chip on red, win; two chips on odd, win; two chips on even, win; two chips on black, lose; two chips on black and one on even, win-win.

Dottie had looked at me, winked and put down two on the number 66 (Route 66 had brought us to California) and *six* on the number 25 (the number of years we had been married at the time). A win on 25! We are both stunned speechless. It takes Dottie a long while to lay hands on the mounds of chips the wheel manager pushes in her direction. She touches the piles tentatively, looking around nervously, like she expects the bells and alarms to go off any second and casino strongmen to rush out and drag her away by her armpits.

From that time on, ignoring the promise we had made to each other, Dottie and I had made annual pilgrimages to Vegas and, after Brad's death, monthly forays to Reno. Early in our fourth decade of marriage, we had begun visiting Golden Gate Fields once or twice a month.

"BON-GOOOOH!" I scream with every molecule of air in my lungs, as I fling the dice against the wall of the upturned box top. I don't hear any explosions on the beach.

"No hits!" Pip cries. "My three against your two now!"

In the next two rounds, neither of us gets a hit. Then she gets a hit and I get a hit. Her two against my one. Through three more rounds of mutual misses we clack and roll without histrionics. Then I get a hit! *Now,* her sole-surviving infantry against my sole-surviving infantry.

"It's down to hand-to-hand now," Pip says dramatically as she takes up two dice and begins methodically shaking them in her tense little fist. "My grenadiers are out of ammo but they're chasing your wounded exhausted guys through the streets with flame throwers."

I wonder for just a moment if in all her pictures with Ulrich she has seen a human body on fire. I try to push back an image from Saint Lo of two men coming out of a Sherman tank that has just been hit by a Tiger shell. Both men are blazing like just-struck matchsticks.

"Hum," I say thoughtfully, "I don't think my guys are out of ammo though. I think all the city blocks are mounds of rubble and my guys are dug into makeshift bunkers and chewing up your grenadiers with this withering triangulated machine gun fire."

My God, I think to myself as Pip continues clacking two dice, *I just said that? Fifty-one dead buddies lost to machine gun fire on the beach that first morning and I had just said that?*

"Wait a minute here," I snap. "Why are you rolling two dice when you've only got one infantry unit?"

A stunned blankness comes over Pip's face. The fisted hand descends slowly. She opens it and looks slack-mouth into her palm.

"How could I be so stupid?" she asks quietly. Her tone is very adult and very earnest, like she has just endangered her only child with her thoughtlessness.

"It happens," I say soothingly. "You're excited. Even the best field commanders make mistakes in the heat of battle."

Pip finally dumps one die. The fisted hand whirls again, the lone die makes a thunk-a-thunk sound inside her cupped palm. She hurls down the die as she screams, "Bongo!"

The die pitches violently against the side of the box and comes to rest with a one right-side-up.

"Yes!" Pip screams.

"Give me that die over there," I snap.

"You have dice over there."

"No, the one you put down when you were trying to throw two. I want that one. It's got a charge to it."

"Yeah, but it's my charge," she says edgily.

"Too bad," I snap. "Give it to me."

With eye slits narrowing Pip hands the die to me. I feel myself glaring back at her but I don't care.

"If I get a hit, everyone's dead but the Caucasus remains mine." I say this harshly, to myself, to pump myself up. "One or two, baby. One or two. One or two and we're home free." I shake the die with a violent vigor. I fling it down into the box top. It whirls up onto one of its points and spins like a dreidel. It spins and spins and spins. I flash on Dottie at the Reno craps table on our fortieth anniversary, waiting for her hundredth throw of the night to settle the question of whether we would pay off the entire balance of our Paloma mortgage.

"FIVE!" Pip screams. "No hit, no hit, no hit! The Caucasus is mine! I own Stalingrad! I own it! I own it!" She throws two fists up into the air, rises from her chair and does an Indian war dance around the table. "The Caucasus oilfields are open to me – I shall have all the fuel my tanks need! I shall be in Moscow by Christmas. Tehran by spring! Cairo by autumn! Yes! Yes! Yes! Yes! *Yes!*"

She is shouting now, marching around the living room like a little conqueror on victory parade. It scares the Dickens out of me. It actually turns my stomach. *A nine-year-old Hitler in my living room.*

My doorbell rings.

"Can you get that?" I say to Pip, desperate for a pretext to calm her down.

"Sure," she says with instant poise. She runs to the door and opens it.

"Oh, it's *you* doing all that screaming," I hear Mary say good-naturedly.

I'm up from the table as quickly as I can move.

"Morning, Mortie."

"Morning, Mary."

"I was just passing by your door after looking in on Chloe Johnson in 516. I heard all this screaming. I thought it might be television but I wanted to make sure."

"Pip and I are playing a board game. She gets very excited when she's whipping my behind. Come on in."

Mary comes right in. She's in her form-fitting exercise sweats and she looks great. "What's the game?"

"Axis and Allies," Pip says excitedly. She's already got Mary's hand and is leading her toward the table. "It's a World War Two game.

I'm the Axis commander. My German forces just took the Caucasus!"

I watch Mary's face as Pip says all this. Her easy confident smile gradually turns to unblinking stone. Her shoulders seize up a little, like a cold wind has just blown past her.

"Hey, maybe you can help great granddad out by taking one of his countries," Pip says. "You could be the British maybe."

"No, no, dear," Mary says quietly but emphatically. "That sort of game isn't for me."

I hear something in her tone. Nothing definite, just very off from her usual in-command-of-everything tone.

"Well, just watch for a while," Pip says. "Maybe you'll get interested after you see the way things work. Okay, great granddad, now watch what I do to your convoys in the North Atlantic."

We play on. Mary stands over the board with her frozen shoulders, with fear in her eyes – no, not fear but rather a haunted sadness. I can look at her quite frankly because her eyes are fixed unblinkingly on the board. But they aren't on the North Atlantic. They are on central Europe where the field gray of the German military swarms over every province.

"Watch your ass!" Pip shouts as she clacks the dice. She's got an audience in Mary now and she's playing to it for all it's worth.

"Bongo!" Pip screams as she throws down the dice – Mary visibly starts with the violence of it.

"Two hits! You're gone, granddad! Both convoys *gone!* Everywhere the Fatherland is triumphant!"

"I must go," Mary says suddenly. "Off for my morning walk up Fillmore," she says, a little impatience lacing her tone. "Can't talk you guys into coming out into the sunshine? It's a beautiful day."

Pip quickly and emphatically speaks for both of us. "No thanks. We're really into this game."

"Okay then," Mary says reluctantly.

I suddenly panic. "Are you having lunch in today?" I say a little desperately.

"No. I have my TAGS work at noon and going well into the early evening."

"See you at dinner then," I say almost pleadingly.

"No, got a date tonight after my TAGS."

A date *tonight*. Last night with us wasn't a real date then.

"See you around then," I manage to say. "Enjoy your day."

She squeezes my forearm tenderly, throws a haunted glance back at the war table and is soon out the door.

Dressing the Battlefield

As soon as I close the door on Mary, Pip says:

"Your turn to defend in the North Atlantic, great granddad. Let's see if your sinking convoys can find the courage to take my wolf packs down with them."

I turn back toward Pip without going back to the table. I'm angry with her now, and tired of this war fever that has driven Mary away. Mary in my room! Right here! I could have offered her something. She might have sat for a while. Pip is clacking practice dice – it's not even her turn anymore -- and giving me this *Come back here and get your beating* sort of look. She is channeling Ulrich in maximum volume. My anger with her turns to a cold shivering revulsion.

"I think we ought to tone down this war fever, Pip. This is a game. Just a game. You understand?"

"You're angry because I'm beating you," she says calmly. "Because Mary saw you losing."

"Stop it," I manage to get out quickly despite my shock.

"I know you like her. You were very, very embarrassed in front of her."

"That's got nothing to do with it!" I snap loudly.

Even though I haven't really shouted at her, even though she is across the room, Pip stumbles backward, as if I've slapped her. We stare at each other for just a moment. Before I can get out *I'm so sorry, honey*, she says:

"You don't have to play with me. It's okay. Ulrich and I will play."

"No," I say quickly, "You and I will play."

"Ulrich and I will play."

"Ulrich will take the Allies' side?" I ask.

It is nonsensical thing to say but I am terrified for her and I have nothing wise to say.

She doesn't answer me. She starts sweeping pieces off the board.

"No, don't," I plead. "I want to go on."

"I'll set it up for Ulrich and me. Ulrich and I will play."

She has said that three times now, each time in the identical dead flat tone, with the cadence of a solemn oath. I go to her. She has stopped sweeping pieces off the board. She clicks on the stopwatch in the baggie and starts putting individual units back into game-start positions all over the board. I kneel beside her and just look at the side of her blank face as she continues. I expect my looking at her to make some sort of impression on her, to break through to her in some way. It doesn't. Finally, I just place my hand on top of hers. She is instantly still. It frightens me that she doesn't fight my touch. That means she expects to hear something from me. Something comforting. Something wise. I have nothing for her. I pray for something. Nothing comes. In my desperation I say something else stupid:

"Ulrich is dead, honey."

No reaction from her. She continues staring blankly at the board.

"You love him very much, I know. And he loves you. He wants you to go on loving him and remembering him without getting trapped."

"Trapped in what?"

"In things that shouldn't matter after a while. He was twelve, right?"

She nods. "He'll be thirteen next month."

"And he was very, very smart, wasn't he?"

She nods. She finally blinks, which relieves me greatly. The blink is like a little hole I've drilled through to her heart. I feel a little empowered to go on.

"Ulrich's mind was just expanding and expanding every day. Eventually he would have been fourteen with all sorts of new ideas and new interests. Then he would have been fifteen and sixteen. He would have put Axis and Allies on his shelf or under his bed or given it away to a younger child or your mother would have sold it in a garage sale. He would have gone on to other things because when you hang on to things that go with being thirteen, you don't get to be all that you can be when you're fifteen or sixteen. Ulrich would have seen that as he grew older because that's just the way life is, honey. We all outgrow things. Now, wherever he is, he wants you to see that too. He wants you to be happy growing up. He doesn't want you to forget him, but he wants you to outgrow him. Outgrow him as you remember him. He just wants you to enjoy more and more of your own life. Because when a brother loves a sister as much as he loved you, that's all a brother wants."

"Do you enjoy more and more of your own life without great grandma Dottie?"

She is so damned calm as she says this. It's a dart to my heart and she knows it – at nine she *knows* this.

"No," I say honestly. "But I think I'm learning to. I can tell you that I feel a lot better about being alive today than I felt a week ago."

"But are you enjoying life more?"

I think. I think about last week, before she was standing at my door for the first time. I think about last month, before Mary sat at my lonely lunch table and introduced herself.

"Yes," I finally say into her expectant eyes. "A lot more."

"Why?"

"Because you are in my life. If I hadn't made room for you in my life I would still be trapped in my grief for great grandma Dottie. When you let grief be the biggest thing in your heart, it blocks out everything else. But when you let some of the grief out, you make room for something else, for more love for other people, for more love *from* other people."

"But when you let go of the hurt for someone who's gone, you're letting them go too. That's not right, is it?"

"You won't ever let go of Ulrich, honey. He's so deep inside your heart that this letting-go can never, ever happen. He's helping to make you smart and strong right now, at this very moment. Do you know that? It's true. He will do that even after you are grown."

"Really?" she says with deep hope, but with her eyes still skeptical.

"Really. Some day you'll have your own children, just like your mom. And you know what? Every time you say something wise or loving to your children, Ulrich will be speaking to them too. That's just the way it is. It's what God gives to us to make our loss of loved ones bearable."

She can't hold my gaze. She looks down at my hand on her and focuses on my band aid. She starts picking at the edges of it.

"He shouldn't have died like that," she says quietly.

"No death is easy, honey. Not a single one of them."

"He shouldn't have died like that," she says again, more quietly. She looks at me as if I could have prevented it. "That was so unfair."

"Yes," I say carefully, "it was –"

"It was unfair!" she screams full blast. "No one should die like that!"

She starts whimpering. With one violent brush of her arm she sweeps the board clean. She pushes the box and the box top off the table. She starts beating the board with her fists. Only when I sense that she is hurting her hands do I finally react to her fury. I catch her hands, and when she pulls away from me yelling I pull her forcefully into me and I don't let go.

She cries for a long, long time, or maybe it just seems that way to me because in my kneeling posture my back and my knees ache something terrible.

Finally, she stops weeping.

I say to her – and I know to say it because I've been thinking about what to say to her when she is calm again, I've actually been *rehearsing* it to keep my mind off my knees: "Do you know the best thing to do when you lose someone?"

"No," Pip says. "What?"

"To love someone else in your life really, really hard. To cling to them and just say 'I love you and I'm so glad you're alive.'"

"That doesn't sound like it'll work."

"It works."

"You did that after great grandma Dottie died?"

Silence.

Finally, I say: "No. No, I didn't. I didn't have anyone to hug and say that to when she died."

"Then what are you talking about? You don't know what you're talking about."

"I know it will work because I feel it in my heart right now. I'm about to say it and I know it will make me feel so much better after I say it…I love you, Pip. I love you so much. I love you with all my heart and I'm so glad that you are in my life."

Her eyes are pure marbled skepticism. But she swallows hard and her lips tremble and in that moment I know that she is desperate to believe me.

"You make my life now," I declare quietly. "I live for our Thursdays together now."

"After just two Thursdays?"

I nod. "Is it all right with you if I ask your mother for Tuesday, Wednesday, Thursday and Friday?"

She can't bear to look into my eyes anymore. She looks at the band-aid again, picks at it.

"Mom says one day a week is a burden for you already. You're old and don't have the energy and patience for me."

"Well, that's what I thought before we met each other. That's not how I feel now. What do you think after a few days with me?"

A long silence yawns between us. She continues picking at my band-aid. "Why do you have so much energy for me now?"

"You find all sorts of things you didn't think you had when you start loving someone."

"I haven't known you very long," she says. "I've seen other kids with their grandparents. They love each other. But you aren't even my grandfather. You're my great grandfather."

"What's wrong with that?"

"Love doesn't stretch that far, does it? I mean, aren't most great grandparents dead before they have to love their great grandchildren?"

"Yeah, they are. But I'm lucky. I am blessed. I get that chance."

"But you're very old," she says matter-of-factly. "You might die soon. Ulrich was only twelve and he died."

"That's just the way it is in this life, honey. There are no guarantees. You know what a guarantee is?"

She nods.

"What is it?" I can't help but press – it's the teacher in me.

"It's a solemn promise to always do something right," she says.

I squeeze her arm, more to fortify myself against tears. "No one can make a solemn promise to keep on living. That just isn't something any of us can do. All we can do is love as much as we can while we're alive and while our loved ones are alive. That's all we have. And you know what?"

"What?"

"It's enough. It really is."

I hug her. She sort of hugs me back. I feel powerful, like I've partially liberated her. Silly me. She gently disengages from me and resumes her setting-up of the game board.

I watch her quietly, assuming that she needs to do something else while she collects her next thoughts on death, loss and grief. I expect us to continue along those lines at any moment now.

"We'll just take a little time now to set everything up for a new game," she says in a lilting sing-song. "Then we should get out into the sunshine, like Mary says."

I hear her pain in the silence but don't see it in her unblinking eyes or steady hands. I begin helping her set up things, my own hands trembling so much I can barely make the infantrymen stand on their feet.

"Only one infantry in western Canada," she says.

Out and About

We spend the bulk of the afternoon out just as Pip decrees. After an Argyll lunch, we take a cab up Telegraph Hill to Coit Tower. We circle the top of the hill drinking our fill of the great revolving views of the Bay, of downtown, the City's hills and the distant counties across the Bay. It's a clear and blustery day. The bridges stand out in metallic clarity against dark blue bay water and azure blue skies. The bay water ripples in the stiff wind and American flags flap vigorously from the flagpoles of dozens of high-rise buildings.

Pip asks me to name every building I can identify, starting with a distant white tower she spots across the Bay.

"The bell tower on the University of California campus," I say.

From that distance the Cal Berkeley campanile is a small white monolith nestled among gray buildings and a scatter-patch of lush green trees. I think of Dottie. I remember our friendly (I thought) argument over just how smart she was. I recall her betting me a hundred dollars that she could get into Cal Berkeley. We were still childless at the time. She applied and got accepted. I think of how much more she could have done with her fine brain if she had gone to Berkeley rather than stayed married to me.

On our side of the Bay, I name all the major downtown commercial buildings that we can see. But juniper trees growing up around the crown of the hill block our view from several vistas. We stroll around the hill to take in unobstructed views of the more residential parts of town. I identify the Fontana, name all the hotels on Nob Hill and most of the condo towers on Russian Hill. I give her the history of Ghiradelli Square. She wants to go up to the observation level in Coit Tower. We go up but the observation level is closed. Our good fortune: the tower custodian happens to be there, happens to overhear Pip's disappointment and he recognizes me.

"Aren't you Mr. Morton Willbanks?" he says.

"I am," I say, momentarily taken aback. No one in a public place has recognized me in years. And my name on the lips of someone outside the Argyll comes as a mild electric shock.

"I'm Gary Tolkien, Mr. Willbanks," the custodian says sticking out a hand. "I'm sure you don't remember me but I was one of your students back in the late seventies. At Wash."

"Gary, I've got to be honest," I say as I take his hand. "I don't remember. Let me blame that on my eighty-year-old brain."

We both laugh.

I say sincerely, "I hope that I did well by you."

"Yeah," he says chuckling, "you were pretty rough on me but you did all right."

We chat for a few minutes. Gary catches me up on the last thirty years of his life in about ten sentences. He married his high school sweetheart and had three children who turned out well. He is terribly complimented when I vaguely recall his sweetheart, a bright but very shy girl named Christine.

"Kristin," Gary corrects me, but he is still stunned. "It's true then: principals never forget a thing."

We laugh heartily.

He's been at Parks and Rec for the past fifteen years and he's very satisfied. I introduce him to Pip who is utterly charming. I am so impressed by her modesty and friendly reserve – so at odds with the foul-mouth sassiness of the world warrior.

Gary opens up the observation deck just for her and then leaves us alone. The view is breath-taking. We see clear to the wine country to the northeast and Silicon Valley to the south. The Marin Headlands are simply a natural glory. Pip wants me to name the downtown business high-rises that are visible to us now. She wants their histories and the names of their architectural styles. I tell her all that I know about the Ferry Building, the B of A building and the Transamerica pyramid.

"Are you interested in architecture?" I ask.

"Sort of," she says. "Ulrich is really interested in it."

She stops herself. She looks out into the distance and shivers. I don't know whether she shivers because of Ulrich or because of the sudden ferocity of the breeze. Charmaine has brought her to me with a light downy jacket that is little better than a padded windbreaker. I take off my jacket and wrap it around her. That warm surrender comes over her face.

"Thank you, great granddad." She says this ever so quietly, without looking at me.

She looks out at the Transamerica building again. "He's got all these sketchbooks full of his ideas," she says. "He's got a building like the Transamerica pyramid, only it's standing on its point. Ulrich says that if you can balance a pyramidal skyscraper on its point, you don't have to spend a lot of money on excavations and piles and foundations and earthquake re-enforcements. He says it would cost a third as much to build a building and you could put it up in half the time. I tell him that doesn't make any sense at all. I tell him the building would just topple over before it was even finished. He says all these electro-magnetic fields will hold it in place. He says he's working on these machines that will keep the electro-magnetic fields spinning around the building, like keeping it in an invisible cocoon." She finally looks up and around at me. "Machines like that can't be made, can they, great granddad?"

"Maybe they can. I think Ulrich was on to something. I think that's a genius idea."

"Really?" she says, squinting skeptically at me.

"Really."

She still is not sure.

We are silent for a long while, each looking over his, her, part of the Bay view. I focus on the flags. I think of my buddies. I shiver a little now. I suppress it so as not to make Pip feel uncomfortable in my jacket. But I'm ready to move on, to jump on the bus that is idling at the bus stop below and just go anywhere that's warm.

"You're right about growing up," Pip says.

I hold my breath – a selfish moment for me: someone on this earth thinks that *I* am right about something? She doesn't look at me; she looks down at my band-aid and starts picking at it.

"Ulrich was growing up, just like you said. He used to play Axis and Allies all the time. Then he got interested in designing things and after that he spent almost as much time with his sketchbooks as he did on Axis and Allies."

"And what would you do when he was with his sketchbooks?"

"I'd draw things too. Clothes mostly. Clothes I'd like to wear. Mom can only afford Goodwill, and sometimes T.J. Maxx. It's okay. Ulrich doesn't mind. But I started designing clothes I'd like to buy when Mom can afford them."

"So Mary taking us to see Vivienne Westwood was really something for you, huh?"

"Yeah," she says without enthusiasm.

"But you didn't tell Mary that you design clothes, did you? It never came up last night."

"I don't really design anything. It's just silliness."

I take hold of the hand picking at my band aid and squeeze it. "You listen to me. Listen. Every thing you do is important. Every thing you say or think or feel or want is important. Because it is you and *you* are special. I bet if you asked Vivienne Westwood when she first began drawing clothes, she'd say, 'Oh, when I was a little girl -- eight or nine or so.' I bet if you asked the architect of the Transamerica building when he first began drawing buildings, he'd say, 'Oh, when I was a kid --seven or eight or so.'" I pull my jacket more tightly around her. She is lost in it. I brush back her hair. Her eyes close. I just look at her, loving her, waiting for her to come back to me. When she returns, I say:

"On the first day of the school year I used to ask my students what they wanted to be when they grew up. And after they told me, I'd say, 'Well, let's get started on getting you there.' You know what?"

"What?"

"The students who worked hard at it grew up to be pretty much what they wanted to be."

"How do you know?" she says insolently.

"Because I stayed in touch with my good students, and they stayed in touch with me."

"So, Mr. Tolkein wasn't one of your good students then."

Alarmed, I look around to make sure Tolkein is out of earshot. I laugh nervously as I squeeze Pip's arms.

"Give me a break here, okay? Just listen. The ones who wanted to become doctors became doctors, the ones who wanted to become teachers became teachers, engineers, engineers, pilots, pilots. They became these things because they took their childhood thoughts and dreams and drawings seriously. You know the smarter you are, the sooner you have to start taking yourself seriously. Because if you don't, a lot of all that smartness just goes bad inside of you. Smartness needs fresh air and sunshine, just like your skin does. If it doesn't get it, it becomes scabby and infected, just like your skin. Pretty soon it becomes a major health problem, instead of something that helps you and nourishes you. You are so very, very smart, Pip. You have no idea how smart you are. I want you to start taking yourself seriously right now, right this very minute."

Her big round eyes have fixed me by now, and they are blazing.

"Right *now*?"

"Right now. And when you come back to me next week, I want you to bring your sketchbooks."

"I don't have any sketchbooks. I just did things on sheets of paper."

"Have you kept the sheets of paper?"

"No."

"Well, it's time to keep sketchbooks. We aren't going home until we buy some at an art supply store somewhere."

Pip grins at me. In an instant she has whipped out her Blackberry.

"Yellow Pages.com can tell us where the nearest one is."

I watch her work her buttons and study her display screen. I want to crush her to me and thank her. I think of her mother. I try to recall one time – just one – when I asked her what she wanted to be or what she feared or how she felt about herself deep down. There is no need to try to recall -- I know it before I start trying. I fight the tears but not the welling sense of self-loathing. I stand up and walk some distance around the observation deck, to hide my eyes.

"Come back here, great granddad," Pip commands. "We've got some choices here."

I go back to her. She says, peering at the screen on her cell phone, "This Utrecht Art Supplies seems to be the closest. On…at 149 New Montgomery Street."

"That little screen tells you all that?"

"Well, yeah," she says in a superior tone. "Just look at it yourself."

"Screen's too small. I can't read that small type. But how did you get all that on the screen in so short a time?"

"Do you now anything about the internet, great granddad?"

"Not a thing."

"Well, don't be so proud of that. An educated man like you – a school teacher, for the love of God."

"Watch your mouth," I grumble.

"Do you even own a laptop?"

"Nope."

"And no cell phone."

"You know I don't," I say, withering.

"Are there computers in the Argyll library?"

"Yes."

"Ever *used* them?"

"Nope."

"We've got to get you into the twenty-first century, man, before you get run over by something contemporary."

"You don't even know the meaning of 'contemporary,'" I say in deep annoyance.

She shakes her head, mildly disgusted. "Well," she says through a sigh, "no more Axis and Allies *for you* until we put in a little computer time."

No *Axis and Allies* for me! She actually means that to be a form of punishment. I laugh.

She doesn't. Then I think: *Yes, I'd rather roll war dice at my sun window table than struggle with a computer in the library.* Five thousand adult voices whom I knew as teenagers roar and laugh at me. I think I hear Gary Tolkien's above all the others.

We ride the bus down to North Beach. I take my jacket back and buy her a thick San Francisco tourist sweatshirt. She runs her hand over the sleeve like a woman runs a hand over the sleeve of her new fur coat. She gives me that look of warm surrender as I re-wrap her in her windbreaker.

"Thanks, great granddad," she says ever so quietly. Those big eyes are glistening pools.

I just can't say, *You're welcome, honey* – I'll break. I start busily adjusting my own jacket to fight back my tears. That's a little hard to do because she puts that three-finger lock on my good hand and won't let go.

We take a cab to New Montgomery Street, near the Financial District. We buy five giant sketchbooks, a smaller traveling one and lots of pens and drafting pencils.

"All the great designers keep their big sketchbooks at home, safe and dry; but they always carry a little notebook with them." I say all this just to say something, to hear the sound of my own great grandfatherly voice.

We take a long walk over to Mel's Diner and have some burgers and chocolate malts. Throughout our little feast Pip stares at me like I'm God in that burning bush. It feels so good. But Pip looks so much like her mother and I am reminded again of failings and unconscionable parental silences in years gone by. Several times I reach across the table to squeeze her little hand, even when it's attached to her malt glass.

We get on a bus just to see where it takes us. We end up at Pier 39. We're strolling around wondering if we have room for caramel pop corn when Pip gets a call on her Blackberry. Charmaine tells her – tells us – that she's getting off early today, that she'll be by at five to pick up Pip and commute back to Hayward. We agree to meet at the Embarcadero BART station instead. From there Charmaine and Pip can just jump on a Hayward-bound train and get home in thirty minutes or so.

As soon I hang up with Charmaine, Pip says to me, "We're meeting Mom before we go back to your place?"

"We won't go back to my place," I say, taken aback by the alarm in her eyes. "We're going to meet downtown at the BART station in about an hour and she's going to take you home from there."

"Then you keep the big sketchbooks," Pip says with some urgency. "Keep them in the bag and pretend like they're yours if she asks about them."

"Why? Don't you want to take them home?"

"No," she says emphatically. "Keep'em at your place. Don't tell her anything."

I stoop down to her. "Why not?"

"She's got enough to worry about."

I don't know what to say. I puff and stutter in confusion. "You don't want her to know that you've got a new hobby? That's nothing for her to worry about, honey. That's a good thing for her to know."

Pip is close to tears now. "She doesn't have the energy to think about anything new, good or bad. Don't you understand? Just do it, great granddad. I know what I'm talking about."

I nod bleakly. "Okay."

I caress her cheek as I study her big troubled eyes. I kiss her. Her eyes go wide and round with a sudden troubling thought.

"You'll keep Axis and Allies up?"

"Just as it is. Ready for us to start a new game."

She thinks. She says earnestly, "After a little computer time, that is."

"Yeah, that too," I say bleakly.

Charmaine is waiting for us at the BART ticket kiosk. After greeting and hugging Pip, she smiles at me warmly and says, "Thanks, granddad. See you Thursday then?"

"I was thinking," I start in a stutter. "Pip and I are so good together. I'd like to take her Tuesday through Friday. She could even stay overnight if you like."

Charmaine is stunned. She smiles down at Pip. "My, some young thing has been charming the pants off her great granddad."

I wince at the metaphorical language, thinking of Charmaine's "charming" teenage years.

"What do you say to that?" Charmaine says, rubbing Pip's cheek. "Would you like that honey?"

"Very much," Pip says.

Charmaine beams at me. "It's so great you two are making a connection," she says to me. "I'll bring a little suitcase of her things on Tuesday then. Thank you – this really helps."

I watch them disappear down the escalator. My heart flies out of my chest when Pip turns back and gives me a little wave.

Later that night, when I return to my room after dinner, I get a call from Charmaine. Without a hello or any lead-in, she says:

"You've been talking to her about Ulrich and *death*? Nothing else on the whole damned planet of things you two could talk about."

"She's grieving, Charmaine. You can't get over Ulrich's *death* without thinking about *death*."

"Don't you dare take that tone with me. I've been a mother for twelve years now. How long since you've been a real father?"

Head shot. I reel in pain, with the instant recollection of the many failures with her and with her mother. But I'm fighting for Pip, I say to myself, so I come back at Charmaine:

"Pip has never gotten a chance to release her grief, to express it out loud and have someone tell her that it's all right to feel such pain. Has she even cried with you?"

"I recall you being a math and English teacher," Charmaine says coldly, "not a child psychologist. I have a regiment of child psychologists working with her. Okay? That's the main reason I'm hanging on to this stupid job, to qualify for a health plan that gets her all the help she needs. So she doesn't need kitchen table help, okay? Okay, granddad?"

"Charmaine, she is ready to grieve. She's ready to open up her wound and let it drain. Let's help her do that."

Silence at her end. Then with ice coldness: "I need you to help us, not to make our lives more complicated. Can you do that *or not?*"

I hear the threat. "I can," I say humbly.

"Then we'll be there Tuesday – and no more talk about Ulrich or death or draining wounds. Clear?"

"Clear."

She hangs up.

Mary on My Couch

The dial tone punctuating the last of Charmaine's words is like a needle in my ear. I slump into a chair and worry about Pip. I start thinking of ways I can maintain the momentum of her progress without violating the agreement I have just made with Charmaine.

My doorbell rings. I have no interest in answering it until the ringer knocks gently.

"Mortie?" I hear Mary ask tentatively from the other side of the door.

I'm up in an old man's flash.

"Hi," she says intimately as I open the door.

"Hi," I say with my heart in my throat.

"Just got back from my date -- well, my date and my TAGS. Thought I'd say goodnight to my favorite nine-year-old."

"She's gone back to Hayward with her mother."

"Oh, that's right – I forgot. Just on Thursdays, right? Today was a bonus."

"Well, starting next week, I'll have her Tuesday through Friday."

"That just great, Mortie," she says, her eyes instantly moistening. "God, that's just great. Congratulations."

"For what?"

"For stretching a little," she says winking. The wink forces a tear to run the side of her nose. She does nothing to it. She stands there in the hallway, nowhere close to moving. The idea occurs to me that she hasn't forgotten at all that Pip was going back tonight.

"Would you like to come in for a while?" I finally say, quaking.

She chuckles. "If I can take my shoes off and put my feet up. I need to get out of these shoes."

She's across my threshold before I fully open the door. She brushes past me on her way to the living room. She smells so good.

"Would you like something to drink?" I say heading for the kitchen.

"Only if it's alcoholic."

I wince, thinking of Dottie: Dottie in Vegas, Dottie in the late afternoons on Paloma Street.

"No," I say. "Sorry, just fruit juices here."

"A glass of anything fruity then," she says.

When I come to her with a glass of apple juice her naked feet are up on the coffee table and her skirt hem is up around her thighs.

"Thank you," she says.

I panic a little. The only chair in the suite of furniture surrounding the coffee table is directly across from her. To spare both of us any embarrassment I sit next to her on the sofa. She sighs heavily as if discharging the last nervous energy from her long day.

"Long day?" I ask.

"Long day," she shoots back instantly. She sighs again. "Lot of pain in the world, Mortie. A lot of young pain."

"I know."

Silence.

I begin thinking that Mary has some sort of wisdom from her TAGS duty that I might bring to bear on Pip's situation. I say as quietly as I can, "Pip's older brother died a few months ago."

"What? Oh, my God."

"They were very close. Very close. He was something of a brilliant recluse, even at twelve years old. He and Pip used to play Axis and Allies all the time. That's why she's so attached to the game. It's the only part of him that she has left – she thinks."

"Oh, Mortie," Mary says tragically. She begins to weep quietly.

We are silent for a long time. After a while longer, she reaches out and takes my hand lying between us on the couch.

"I can see it now," she says. "You did some kind of job with her yesterday. Yes, some kind of job, Mortie."

"I didn't do much of anything."

"Yes, you did. Just the right touch at every moment. Where did you get it from?"

I try to shrug away a sudden welling of depression. "Whatever it is that you think I have, I wish I'd had it with her mother. Or her grandmother, or her great uncle."

That all piques her interest. I tell her the whole sad tale, from Dottie's first joyous pregnancy with Brad right up to the moment that I hang up with Charmaine this evening. Mary is silent for a long while. The ambient light from the outside streams in and illuminates her sad face. It dawns on me finally that I've not turned on any lights. She reads my mind as I move to get up.

"No, don't turn on any lights," she says. "Darkness is nice. It's very soothing."

I settle back into the couch, my eyes on her thighs which seem to glow in the ambient light.

"I am just so exhausted," she says. "Doubt that my feet will get me to my own door, especially if I have to wedge them back into those shoes."

"Your place is right upstairs," I insist. "Maybe a hundred steps from this couch. Elevator will do all the work."

What a stupid thing to say. What a damned *stupid* thing to say. The ensuing silence seems to agree with me. Good Lord, I'm seven decades past puberty and that's the best I can do with this opening of an opportunity that is so damned wide I could drive a truck through it?

Still the silence. I think she's giving me time to make a reasonable comeback. But then I think, *Why should I think that -- why?* I remember her lovers. Even the ones in their fifties have their full heads of hair and their shoulders so much broader than their waist lines. Secure in the darkness, I pinch my crotch, not out of any erotic impulse but out of a deeply punitive and self-hating one. *You don't deserve what little you've got left.*

I'm not one of those rogue widowers, I tell myself. That's why I'm suddenly stupid: it's self-defense. Yes, that's right. I don't want to replace Dottie in my bed or in my heart. I miss her so much. I miss her warmth, even the warmth generated by her scotches and brandies.

Too much time passes. Curdled memories consume most of it. Second chances evaporate. Mary gets up and goes to the bathroom on naked feet but carrying her shoes. She's gone quite a while. When she comes out she goes to the entry way and flips on the light switch. Her clothes are once again immaculately neat and she's got her shoes on. The usual mischievous twinkle in her eyes is gone. In its place: the dullness of thwarted intention. I'm sure of this. *You did have a chance! You idiot!*

I rise pretty athletically and go to her. On my way there, I assure myself that I will do something pretty dramatic when I arrive. But by the time I arrive, her back is to me and her hand is on the door handle.

"Night, Mortie. Thanks for the juice and the companionship."

"Good night, Mary," I say weakly.

I stand on my threshold and watch her move down the hall. She is tired but she moves with deliberate grace. There is no limp to her gait. Those shoes don't pinch her in the least. I'm sure she means for me to know that.

I am a stupid old man and I feel every one of my years.

Circling the Board

Another "longest" weekend of my life. I don't do much except walk around my apartment thinking of Mary and sit in my easy chair thinking of Pip. I play the game of trying to recall a longer weekend. The one last week when I nearly died for lack of Pip's company? The one in Antwerp waiting for that transport ship which takes me home after the war? The one preceding Brad's very late birth on that dreary Monday morning in 1948? The one when Dottie left me for all of seventy-four hours of a "trial separation?" I wither more with every recollection and every passing hour.

  I don't go down to the dining room for any of my weekend meals. I claim illness and have them all sent up to me. I'm too afraid of running into Mary, terrified that Dick-less Old Me will have to walk past Mary's table where she is entertaining one of her fifty-year-old lovers.

On Sunday afternoon, I begin to fret with nervous anticipation of Pip's arrival on Tuesday morning. I find myself circling the *Axis and Allies* board with a faint pleasure. I survey the game-start troop dispositions and debate various strategies for assuring that the Soviet Union survives Pip's initial onslaught. I draw up contingency plans for an early cross-Channel invasion of France if Pip's Germans get too caught up in Karelia and the Caucasus. It is easily an hour before I realize that I have done these things nonstop without thinking of my lost ones on the beach, at Saint Lo, or in the Ardennes. I realize that this is not so much progress in some sort of healing process as it is a desperate need to relive moments with Pip, to make her presence as tangible as possible. I try to conjure up an image of her standing on the other side of the table, trying to intimidate me with one of her Ulrich war stares, unnerving me with one of her Bongo screams. In one of those conjuring moments an epiphany crashes into me: I miss her like she misses Ulrich; I need this game like she needs it, and for the very same reasons. Only she will be here for me in thirty-six hours and Ulrich is in his grave.

I sit down and cry for her, my first free-flowing tears since that last night on Paloma Street in my lonely widower's bed.

A new dream comes to me Monday night. I sit comfortably in darkness. I feel naked but I do not touch myself to confirm this. I hear dice clack incessantly and other dice tumble violently into a card board box. A wall of light flicks on and illuminates the room in which I sit. Crisply uniformed men fill a hundred folding chairs arranged around me in neat rows. Each man stares straight ahead into the wall of light. An image appears on the wall: a sandy beach shrouded by roiling smoke. Soldiers lie on the beach desperately digging into the sand like burrowing dung beetles desperate to avoid sunlight. One of the beach soldiers blows up, his arms flying one way, his legs another. Instantly, a man in the audience jumps up and snaps smartly to attention. Another beach soldier explodes, his numerous parts thrown up into the air – another soldier in the audience jumps up, snaps to attention and salutes crisply. Another brutal image on screen, another man jumps up. One after another – image, man, image, man -- in ever-faster succession, until all are standing and mutely saluting the beach. Only I remained seated, surrounded by a phalanx of uniformed men so dense that the light is blotted out and I am once again in a cool comfortable darkness.

I wake up from the cool darkness. My room is dark and cool and for a moment I look around for the men. They are not there but their intense muteness envelops me like my bed sheet. My heart races a little but my skin, for once, is dry. I lie there quietly awaiting the usual tears, like an epileptic calming himself before an inevitable episode. But no tears come and, wonder of wonders, I fall back into a dreamless sleep.

Deal With It.

On early Tuesday morning Charmaine and Pip show up at my door. Pip marches right in carrying a little pink suitcase. She looks so fresh and healthy that I know that she's had a good weekend. Charmaine looks exhausted and frazzled. She spouts a few words of civil greeting and gratitude but doesn't even cross the threshold. She's moving down the hall in no time.

"I'll call you this evening, honey," she says back over her shoulder.

Pip either doesn't hear her or doesn't care. By the time I close the door she is already standing over the board dressing her battle formations.

"Good weekend?" I ask.

"It was all right," she says.

I don't bother to probe as to what she did and what made her weekend all right. I see those big eyes sweeping over the board and I want to concentrate on them, to glean any clues from them as to what she's planning.

"Okay, let's go," she says.

"A surprise for you today, my little friend," I say with relish. "Something new and refreshing from the Union of Soviet Socialist Republics!"

She looks at me patiently. "*No*," she says. "I meant, now that I've looked the board over, let's head up to the library."

I've got a hundred reasons why we can't go just now – I don't feel like getting out, I don't feel like getting dressed for the Argyll world, the library is a little cold, my eyes aren't up to the strain of looking at a computer monitor. I'm on my fifth excuse when she is standing on the threshold of my open door with her arms crossed, looking at me like I'm her whiny child having a small tantrum. There's a moment of silence, a stand-off devoid of tension because the outcome is inevitable. I go to empty my bladder, put on a cardigan and slip into my best loafers.

We share the elevator going up with several female residents in sweat suits and sneakers. I've seen all of them around the place but I really don't know any of them. For some reason, they all become utterly ecstatic when they discover that Pip is taking me up to the library to teach me how to use a computer and access the internet.

"What a brilliant girl!" one lady says, glowing at Pip.

"And so loving with her granddad!" another says, stroking Pip's hair.

"Actually, he's my *great* grandfather," Pip says.

The extra generation just adds more luster to the wide-eyed regard in which the women hold me.

"A vigorous great grandfather," the third woman mutters.

I hear something inappropriate in her tone. I study her for a long second and belatedly recognize her as one of Mary's nut-case dinner buddies. She looks me up and down like she has met her next cheeseburger.

"I'm going to teach him how to use Google Earth and Google Street View too," Pip blazes on. "Have any of you seen what the Argyll looks like from a hundred feet in the air? Do you ever wonder what your old house looks like right now?"

The women are just astounded. The elevator opens on the fourteenth floor, the floor for the exercise center where they are obviously headed. As they get off, one of them says to Pip:

"I bet you could give us a little seminar on the internet, couldn't you?"

"Sure!" Pip says.

"Morton, we should discuss this later," the woman goes on. "I'm serious. Easily fifty people would show up for this." She winks at Pip as she adds, "I'm sure there's money in the library budget for a little stipend."

"Sounds good," I say as the doors close on them.

"RE –AL –LY?" Pip shouts at me, grinning violently. "Me teaching old people! I can do that! I can just *totally* do that!"

"I'm sure you can."

"What's a stipend?" she says through a sudden frown.

"It's the money you and I would earn for your teaching effort."

"Wow, they'd pay me?"

"Us," I say, smiling. "We're a team."

"Yeah, we are."

She takes three of my fingers and smiles up at me with such loving tenderness.

"Thirty minutes of this," I say as the elevator doors open on the library floor. "It's all I can take."

Thirty-five minutes later (the less said about the computer lesson, the better), we are back in my place. We play for three hours. The dark forces of Fascism surge and recede in all parts of the world. They attack. I throw them back. I feint, they respond with defensive moves which force them to defer new invasions.

"You've been studying things," she says to me with an unblinking glare, after her third failed attempt to take Moscow.

"Yeah," I smirk. "Deal with it."

"*Deal with it?* Where'd you learn that?"

"I'm old, dear heart. Not dead."

"Well, you're certainly dead in England."

But I'm not. The Brits hold with fighter re-enforcements from America. She is downright angry. She says nothing but I see anger in her big brown eyes. She simmers in calm silence and plays on rather brilliantly. The bells of Saint Mary's Cathedral start bonging the noon hour and summoning the faithful to a mid-day mass. It dawns on me in the middle of the twelve bongs that not once have I heard Pip scream "Bongo!" when throwing her battle dice. And I have only had to watch my ass twice in the sixty-odd battles we have fought that morning.

"Let's go down for some lunch," I say, feeling very pleased with myself.

She looks up at me with this patient patronizing gaze.

"Let's wait an hour, if you don't mind, great granddad." She says this ever so politely. "Things are getting a little bit complicated here."

Yeah, because I'm whipping your ass.

Just then someone knocks at the door. My heart immediately races. I go to the door.

"Afternoon, Mortie!" Mary says brightly.

"Good afternoon," I say, mustering up a casual tone.

"Did Pip make it in this morning?"

"She sure did!" Pip says running up to the door.

"Why don't we have lunch together?"

"Great!" Pip squeals. "Just a minute!"

She runs back to the table, studies the board urgently, memorizing the troop dispositions, blowing on the dice as she does so. Meanwhile, I stand awkwardly at the door with Mary. I don't invite her in. I'm too embarrassed. She remembers too.

"It's all right, Mortie," she says. "Don't give it another moment's thought," she adds comfortingly.

That annoys me. I want to step into her and plant one on her mouth, to let her know I'm not some wet dish rag. But that moment passes. Pip is by our side now.

"Okay, let's go!" she says.

Let's go! is the beginning of a wonderful three days. Each day, we three have breakfast together; Mary then goes off to do whatever Mary does in the world of Mary; Pip and I go back up to fight over the world for several hours;

Mary shows up for lunch on two of those days; we go off together on some really fun excursion – a matinee in an art house, a rehearsal session of some new experimental play, a visit to a private residence whose owner Mary has known for years and who has some really choice pieces of art (the owner always being a male who has that goofy-eyed glow on his face, even if he's gay); we return to the Argyll; Mary goes off again while Pip and I return to my place where I take a much-needed nap and she – always to my surprise and delight – pulls out a sketchbook and works while I sleep.

"You mustn't peek in my book," she says every single day. "I'll show you when I'm ready to show you."

"Of course," I say, a little wounded by her lack of confidence in me.

I sleep until dinner time. As soon as I walk out into the living room Pip hurriedly closes her sketchbook and puts it away. She always looks at me with great discomfort, like I have inadvertently seen where she has hidden her treasure and fears that I'll dig it up as soon as she's out of sight. It is Thursday late afternoon before I think to ask:

"Does your suitcase have a lock on it?"

"Yes, a combo lock."

"Well, lock it in your suitcase then. An artist has a right to her privacy."

"Yeah," Pip says in revelation. As she goes to her suitcase she says, "We'll go a few turns at Axis and Allies before we go down to dinner." She smiles lovingly at me. She means *Axis and Allies* to be my reward for respecting her privacy. I sigh.

Mary knocks on our door – we both know it's her by now, we know her knock, she doesn't use the doorbell anymore.

Pip runs to the door. She says preemptively, "Great granddad and I are going to do a round of Axis and Allies before we go down to dinner. Can you come in and just watch us for a while?"

That haunted sadness comes into Mary's face. "I suppose," she says neutrally.

Pip takes Mary's hand and leads her to the battle table. "Japan's turn," she says to me.

I watch Mary as Pip moves her Japanese pieces, providing a running commentary to Mary as to what she has in mind and how this or that particular troop movement will further her aims. I see Mary's distress growing. As Pip finishes moving and starts picking up dice, Mary walks around to Pip's side of the table and takes her by the shoulders. She caresses Pip's hair and stares narrowed-eyed at the crown of her head.

"Wait a minute here," Mary says slowly, as if giving time for some sort of revelation to percolate in her.

"What?" Pip and I say almost in unison.

"You come with me, young lady – Mortie, you cool your heels here. We'll be back in an hour or so."

They leave. I lie down to grab another hour of sleep, figuring that I'll need it for an evening with the two women. I slip into unconsciousness casting about for some sort of move I can make that evening to show Mary that I've still got some lead in my pencil.

A knock at the door. I look at my watch. An hour and a half has passed since I put my feet up! I had gone right out and never stirred. I get up and open the door. They stand there grinning – Pip with this, this stunningly wonderful haircut that makes her look like a child version of Audrey Hepburn. Her hair is the exact color of her bright brown eyes and her face has a scrubbed-clean sheen to it that is so compelling without being provocatively adult-like. She is so beautiful. I mean she's just gorgeous.

Pip walks right past me like a fashion model with an attitude. She gets to the center of the living room, does a runway pirouette and says to me, "Well, great granddad?"

"I'm Morton Willbanks, miss," I say solemnly. "I'm very pleased to make your acquaintance."

They laugh. It's the wittiest thing I've said in decades but I don't dwell on it.

"Kerry did a fine job, didn't she?" Mary says proudly, as if she herself had done it. "Nobody in the beauty parlor wanted to let her go. Cu Raley and her gang came out of the movie theatre as we were finishing up and they just clustered around the parlor gawking at Pip. They kept asking who she was – was she Pip's twin sister dressed up in Pip's clothes?"

Pip is grinning so brightly I want to cry.

Mary declares that the Argyll dining room just isn't good enough for us tonight, that we should get out and strut our stuff. Pip changes into a denim skirt with a regular blouse and a denim waist jacket and we head out for this dive of a restaurant that Mary knows on the edge of Union Square. The place is a dump but the food is excellent. We go through a huge platter of fried calamari and two baskets of lightly-toasted sourdough bread before we even look at our rather greasy menus. It's the most I've eaten at one sitting since Dottie's outrageously extravagant Thanksgiving feasts some decades before. I even share a carafe of wine with Mary, who precedes that with what she calls a "pop" – a neat vodka gimlet with a lip of salt. During the long sitting, Pip goes to the ladies' room several times, to give everyone in the restaurant a second and third and fourth chance to see her new hairdo. Afterward, Pip decides that she wants to walk around Union Square, to see how many more looks of admiration she can garner from passers-by there.

We've strolled around in the square for fifteen minutes when I see Charmaine and a well dressed man coming in our direction from the Hotel St. Francis side of the Square. I'm immediately struck by how much younger he looks than she does. She doesn't see us at first. She is laughing and seems to have an intimate hold on the man's arm. As she comes closer, the embarrassment of recognizing me spreads over her smooth face and wrinkles it deeply. Her eyes flit nervously between Pip and me.

"What are you doing out?" she says to me a little indignantly.

"Oh," I say, drawing out the word, "we get out on the town now and then."

Pip grins. "Hi, mom," she says sarcastically.

Charmaine struggles for seconds with open-mouth shock. Her disconnect between the logical necessity of the young girl with me having to be Pip and the stunning hair style that could not possibly be a part of her daughter finally collapses. "Pip?" she actually says with sincere tentativeness.

"Yeah," Pip says proudly.

"Why are you – what happened to your hair?"

"It's the new me!" Pip exclaims. She steps away from us, dramatically throws out her arms and pirouettes with enough velocity to make her skirt hem twirl around her thighs.

"Who did that to you?" Charmaine says in a demanding tone.

"My new friend did it for me," Pip says. She is grasping Mary's hand now and pulling her forward.

"Hi, Charmaine," Mary says with her usual easy intimacy. She sticks out the hand that Pip isn't grasping. "I'm Mary Givens, one of Mortie's neighbors at the Argyll. I'm so glad to meet you finally."

"Finally?" Charmaine says rather indignantly. She fixes me with something close to a hate-stare. "Like I've been missing in action?"

I look coolly at her. I smile sweetly at her date.

"Hi, I'm Paul Castlerock," the date says fulsomely, thrusting out a nervous hand.

"Yes, Paul is actually my boss," Charmaine says much too loudly. "We've just finished with a company banquet at the St. Francis and he's seeing me to BART."

"Do you have to rush off?" Mary says ever so smoothly. "Let's spend a little time together – maybe we can go up to the Starlite Room and have a slow nightcap."

"I don't want my daughter around alcohol," Charmaine says sniffishly.

"Well," Mary says chuckling, "she's been around it all evening and her hair hasn't fallen out yet. She can have a Singapore Sling, can't she?"

"I'll determine what my daughter can and cannot have, thank you. I'm not rearing an alcoholic."

Awkward silence.

Charmaine seems hurt that everyone is looking at her as if she's made a fool of herself. "Pip should be in bed this time of night anyway," she grumbles.

The boss-date coughs. Charmaine looks at him like he has stabbed her.

"You're right," I say softly. "I've kept her out too long tonight. We'll be on our way home now." I nod in the direction of Castlerock. "Pleased to have met you, Paul."

"And you," he says subdued.

"I'll come by in an hour or so and get her," Charmaine says as she cuts a nervous eye toward her boss-date. "You'll have her ready?"

"Come on, it's only Thursday," I say lightly. "You promised her to me through Friday evening. Look, Pip is having a great time with us and I just can't bear to part with her right now. Let me keep her over the Memorial Day weekend – if she wants to be with me, that is."

"Oh, yes, please!" Pip pipes up.

"We can talk Monday late afternoon," I say. "I look at her boss-date as I add, "After you've had a refreshing three days all to yourself."

Charmaine stares at me as if I'm trying to trick her in some way, as if I want to embarrass her in front of her boss.

"I can't go three days without her," Charmaine says.

She bends down to Pip and tries to kiss her on the cheek – Pip pulls back. Charmaine quickly brushes at Pip's cheek as if wiping away a smudge, as if that was all she had intended to do in the first place.

"I'll call you tomorrow morning, okay, hon?" Charmaine says in a tone of brittle maternal caring. "See what you and great granddad are up to for the day. Maybe he can bring you downtown and we can have lunch together. "

"I don't think so," Pip says flatly. "Our Axis and Allies game is getting really interesting. Great granddad is making a real game of it now. We'll probably play all day."

"Axis and Allies?" the boss-date echoes. "You play that? I played that when I was a kid. How old are you?"

"Nine," Pip says aggressively.

"Wow," the boss-date says. "I didn't get into that game until I was twelve or so. You must be really smart."

"Not really," Pip says. "My brother plays internet Axis and Allies with kids in Japan and France. Some of them are eight."

"Maybe, the three of us can play sometime – you and your brother can be the Allies against my Axis."

Pip says nothing, just stares at her mother who is biting her lip and fighting sudden tears.

"Let's talk Sunday," I say quickly to Charmaine as I try to usher Pip and Mary away. I look at the boss-date, this time mustering what I hope is a respectful mien. "Very pleased to have met you, Paul."

"You too," the boss-date says, relieved.

My last glance over my shoulder as I turn away is of Charmaine glaring right through me. The three of us start walking in the general direction of the Argyll. Pip starts skipping along some distance ahead of Mary and me. Mary takes my arm.

"Cab in front of the Sir Francis Drake?" Mary says. "My feet have started acting up."

"Yeah," I say.

"You've got some cleaning up to do back there."

I swell with annoyance. "I'd say that she's the one with some cleaning-up to do. Did you see how young that guy is?"

"What's that got to do with anything?" she cracks sharply.

"Jesus," I seethe. "From one extreme to the other. She was all over thirty-year-old men when she was seventeen. Now that she's thirty-six, she's hot for teenagers."

"Paul is not a teenager."

"Not by much he isn't."

Like a fighter-bomber locked in on a ground target, Pip suddenly wheels around and swoops down on us. "You talking about my mom?"

"No," I say.

"Yes," Mary says almost simultaneously.

"What were you saying?"

"Mortie?" Mary says leadingly.

I could strangle Mary right now, right here in Union Square with the whole damned world watching, I really could. I manage to push out: "We were just wondering…"

"Wondering what?" Pip says, taking three of my fingers.

"Whether your mom has enough time in life to enjoy her friends," Mary says lightly.

"Her boyfriends, you mean?"

"She has more than one?" I say, trying to filter the shock and the judgment out of my tone.

"Not these days. Just Paul I think. She really likes him."

"But you hadn't met him before tonight, had you?"

"No. But he's Paul. He calls a lot. He's her phone-sex boyfriend."

My heart stops. It just stops, and I stop breathing. Mary actually giggles.

"What do you know about phone-sex?" Mary asks with amused skepticism.

"Just what Ulrich used to tell me. Mom feels a lot better after she and Paul talk."

I sense Mary drawing breath to have a full-blown conversation on the subject and I squeeze the living hell out of her arm to shut her up. Thankfully, the display windows of Saks Fifth Avenue are now in sight across Post Street.

"Wow," I say, "looks like they've changed the displays at Saks. I see some little girl mannequins."

"Really?" Pip says breathlessly. She's off like a shot.

"Don't cross without us!" I shout.

But the pedestrian crosswalk light is green and she scampers across Post Street on her own.

In the elevator going up, Pip stands between us again holding our hands. This is routine for her now and I feel so good about bringing this little vignette of stability into her life. The elevator stops on the fifth floor. Pip turns to Mary and prompts her to stoop down. They kiss.

"Good night," Pip says.

"Good night, honey. Sleep well."

Mary looks at me, a faint smile on her full red mouth.

"Good night, Mary," I say quickly. "Thank you for everything – it's been a great day for us."

"You are so welcome, Mortie. Good night."

Pip and I get off. Pip looks back and gives Mary a final wave but I keep walking.

"Breakfast tomorrow?" Pip suddenly exclaims at the nearly closed doors.

"Yes!" Mary exclaims back through the crack.

As she catches up with me Pip asks, "Why didn't you and Mary kiss good night?"

"Is that really your business, Miss Sassy Nose?"

"She kissed you good night the first night we went out."

"Enough from you, young lady."

"You're shy."

"I am not," I snap.

"You are," she says grasping my fingers. "But that's all right. For now."

The Next Day

Early the next morning, Friday, while Pip is still sleeping, I slip out of my apartment with her cell phone and I call Charmaine. I quickly apologize for any awkwardness the night before and preemptively apologize for keeping Pip out late.

"Your boss seems a really fine man," I say.

"He is," she says flatly. "You didn't need to treat him like dirt."

"Like dirt? I hardly treated him in any way at all."

"Exactly," she says bitterly. "And you didn't need to embarrass me in front of him. You didn't need to make me feel like I'm some sort of office slut creeping around with my boss after dark and neglecting my daughter."

I've got no sympathy for her at all because I recall how she had tried to make Pip feel bad about her new hair style.

"That was never in my thoughts, Charmaine. If anything, I have exactly the opposite thoughts about you and your situation."

"What do you mean, my situation?"

"Well, seeing you out on a date –"

"It was not a date," she seethes.

"Seeing how embarrassed you were made me really feel for you. You probably find it impossible to get a little time to yourself. You know: time to be a healthy single woman with a social life. Would it help if I took Pip a couple of weekends over the rest of the summer? If you use the time to enjoy yourself – to relax and replenish your morale – I wouldn't mind at all."

Silence. I'm sure she is running through all the possibilities of how I might be tricking her.

"That would be great," she finally says, without a hint of gratitude. "But Pip would probably miss me terribly."

"Well, it's for a short period of time – just the rest of the summer. Anyway, she's become really good friends with Mary Givens who is showing her the town in a big way. Bistros, movies, museums, music concerts, private home-showings of world class art. Next week, we're all going to summer symphony pops -- twice."

"I don't much like that woman," Charmaine rumbles.

"Charmaine, come on, what's not to like? Mary is making Pip grow by leaps and bounds and Pip just adores her."

"Yeah," Charmaine says emphatically, as if I've just argued her point for her.

I panic. "Charmaine, how many people in Hayward are introducing your daughter to symphony music, jazz, blues, hip-hop, Chinese installation art, French Impressionism and German Expressionism this summer?"

"You get out for all that?" Charmaine says in a surly sarcastic tone.

I can't help but laugh. "Charmaine, it's a surprise to me too. I didn't think I had it in me – but I have it in me for Pip's sake."

Charmaine thinks about it. Her spinning wheels fill the long silence. "Well, thanks for the weekend offer, but I can't go that long without her. Let's stay with Tuesdays-through-Fridays. Okay?"

Now I am silent. It's her kind of silence, a tactical one.

"Okay, granddad?"

"It's the Memorial Day weekend this weekend," I say in a calm deliberate tone. "I think you and Paul should enjoy each other and leave Pip and me alone."

"Hah!" Charmaine bursts good-naturedly. "Really now. Really. Someone found his old parental chops when he was cleaning out a closet, huh?"

I laugh, relieved. "Could I have her? She doesn't have a psychiatrist appointment on Memorial Day Monday, does she?"

"No," Charmaine says softly. "Yeah, you can have her. But you are always to be with her. Understand? I don't want Pip alone with strangers. She is never to be alone with strangers, male or female."

"Fine."

"I'll bring over some more things for her tomorrow on my way into work."

"Don't bother yourself. I'll buy her whatever she needs."

"I can't afford that."

"It's all a gift, Charmaine. No. No, I won't lie: it's not a gift at all; it's my 'thank you' to you for letting me spend time with Pip."

"She really likes you," she says, in a tone that strikes me as confusion tinged by resentment.

She really likes you for some reason. I can't understand why. I didn't expect that to happen when I tried to dump her on your tired old ass for the whole summer.

I don't trust Charmaine with my new core. I still don't trust her to hear me say, *I love that little girl. I can't live without her now.*

Instead I say: "Yeah. That's strange, huh?"

Watch Out, Vivienne Westwood!

I go back up to my apartment. Pip is still in bed but now she has her sketchbook out. She's sitting up against a banquette of pillows with her knees drawn up as an angled desk on which her sketchbook rests. She eyes me cautiously as I stand at the bedroom threshold.

"You take my Blackberry?" she says.

"I did. Called your mom to see if I could keep you this weekend."

Pip just glows. But she swallows hard. "Like me that much?"

"Yeah, sorta. Hard at work already, huh?"

"I've got ideas," she says cautiously.

"Let's go down for breakfast first. Great art is nourished by good food."

"You just make that up?" she says, already impressed.

"Yeah, I did."

"Cool."

She gets up and starts pulling fresh clothes out of her suitcase. "Is Mary eating with us?"

"Don't know. Let me call her."

When I do call her, Mary says, "I was just about to call you guys. See you in the dining room."

I tell Pip. She is thrilled. "Is it okay if I take one of my sketchbooks to breakfast?"

"Sure," I say.

It soon becomes clear why she wants to. The first thing Mary says after we meet in the dining room and exchange good morning greetings is, "What cha got there? Are you an artist?"

"It's my sketchbook," Pip says, her big brown eyes inviting Mary to probe further.

Within seconds, the sketchbook is open and Pip is giving us both a tour of her creative mind. Most of it is little-girlish stuff rendered with good draftsmanship. But some significant part of it is downright brilliant, ready for the City's kiddy boutiques right now. I can't believe it. Mary is stunned. She lasers in on several pages. Finally, she shakes her head, as if trying to clear away a concussion.

"We're going to refine some of this," she says in a resolute tone. "We're going to polish it and we're going to copyright it if we can. Then we're going to get it in front of *someone's* eyes."

I think that she's being over-the-top encouraging to Pip. I worry when Pip's eyes widen expectantly.

"You've got contacts in the fashion industry?" I ask rhetorically. I'm sure that skepticism is curling my smile.

"Yes," Mary says. "Three of my former lovers are quite involved in the business. One is a fashion photographer for the big magazines. Another has a prêt-a-porter house in Tribeca."

Pip's eyes go round as quarters. I'm not sure whether she's reacting to the sudden vista of opportunities or to Mary's child-inappropriate reference to her romantic career. I know what I'm focused on. *Three of?* How long does *that* list have to get before one ends up with three ex-lovers in the same specialized industry? For long moments, for some reason, I pray that all three are male.

I dare not invite any follow-up details from Mary, not with Pip there. Anyway, Mary and Pip quickly circle the wagons and talk only to each other. I have to remind them that we're here for breakfast and things will start closing down soon. Mary declares that the three of us must spend the morning in the boutiques on Hayes Street and on Grant Avenue.

"Then," she says, "we should swing by Union Square and check out a couple of adult stores on Maiden Lane. Get a frame of reference as to what young girls expect to grow into even as their moms are buying Pip's clothes."

Pip's clothes. Mary says it so matter-of-factly. Pip grins from ear to ear and swells with self-importance. I'm relieved when she falls right in with Mary's program for the day – when she doesn't insist on a few hours of *Axis and Allies* first.

Mary is so anxious to get out that she will not wait for the Argyll house car to return from its normal morning run of taking residents to clinics and hospitals. We pile into a cab.

Mary shows Pip through virtually every store which sells clothes, child and adult. Browsing and window-shopping eventually descend into full-blown shopping. Mary and Pip together pick out four really nice outfits, two of which mimic Pip's current ragamuffin style of dress and two which really show off the mature young woman in her. While trying on various mature outfits, Pip looks at herself in the mirror like she's looking at a strange girl whom she very much wants to befriend but isn't sure how to approach.

Mary grasps my arm and says, "Look at her, Mortie. Isn't she a jewel? Now, you tell me she doesn't like herself a little bit more now than she did when she woke up this morning."

Mortie.

I don't even look at Pip. I look at Mary who, so fixed on Pip, is oblivious to my stare. Every part of me warms. Despite my miserable performance last week I'm still her Mortie.

I call on Dottie, not so much to defend me against myself but as a test of my comfort with my feelings for Mary. I'm entirely comfortable. I squeeze back on Mary's arm. I take hold of her elbow like it's mine, like it's an extension of my body and I need to keep it close by. Mary reacts like it's the most natural thing in the world – that is to say, she doesn't react at all. She's too fixed on Pip, savoring her own handiwork as a Pygmalion.

All the shopping and flitting about makes us all hungry despite the recent huge breakfast. Mary takes us to another one of her special places where the sanitary regime is questionable and the food is mouth-wateringly good. We order a fourth entrée and split it. Afterward, Pip orders this pastry-and-ice-cream concoction that must equal at least a quarter of her body weight.

At our last store visit of the day Mary and Pip decide on a fifth outfit. Mary and I argue over who will pay.

"It's my turn," she says.

"No, you won't. I'm paying – for everything."

Up until then we have compromised: we've alternated with each outfit, one of us paying for the clothes and the other one paying for shoes and accessories. But I won't compromise on this last one. I feel a need to punctuate Pip's great day with my exclusive great grandfatherly stamp of generosity. I have to pull the great grandfather card on Mary. I think that the firmness in my voice excites her a little. Maybe she's just pleased to hear a little progress in me after the weak-kneed mushiness I've shown to her.

We take a cab back to the Argyll to dump all the shopping bags in my room. The bags no sooner hit my sofa than Pip is eyeing *Axis and Allies* over on the sun window table. I brace for the summons to battle. I see Mary tense up in anticipation as well. But Pip surprises both of us. She turns to me and asks, "Could we eat out again tonight? Somewhere where lady diners dress up for the evening?"

"Yeah, let's do it!" I say looking at Mary.

"That would be so nice, honey," Mary says to Pip, "but I'm headed out of town for the weekend. I'm leaving in about half an hour."

"Where are you going?" I ask, trying to keep the sudden sense of abandonment out of my tone.

"Yountville. My father is in the VA home out there. You know that, Mortie. Two weekends a month I drive out there and spend the weekend with him."

"Spend it how?" Pip asks, her disappointment nakedly apparent in her tone. "What do you do with him?"

"Well, this is Memorial Day weekend, so we'll do some special things. This evening I'll take him for a long meal in a fancy restaurant in Saint Helena. Then we'll go to my friend's place outside of Calistoga. He and his wife do this illegal fireworks thing every Memorial Friday. It's such a kick. Dad just lights up. On Saturday, we'll go to Oakland for a baseball game. The Red Sox are in town. Dad's favorite team going back to the war years. Then we go for barbecue in Jack London Square, if he's up for a long day. On Sunday, we'll have a little ceremony over one of the graves in the little veterans' cemetery there. We pick a grave. We pray for the man's soul, for his family; and dad has a long conversation with the man's spirit. Then we go to the VA chapel for noon service. Then we have a blow-out brunch with live band music in the VA cafeteria. After his nap, I'll get him out for a long ride in the country – he loves that. Sometimes we drive to Lake Hennessey or Lake Berryessa and just sit on the shore throwing stones in the water. And on Monday, I'm going to bring him back this way so that he can visit a couple of his buddies in the VA cemetery in San Bruno."

"Which war did he fight in?" Pip says in awe.

"World War Two. And a little of Korea."

"In France?" Pip exclaims.

"He did, as a matter of fact. Sicily, France, Germany. You'd probably love talking to him."

"Yeah, I would! Did he kill a lot of Germans?"

Mary turns sadly solemn. Ever so quietly she says, "You never want to ask a veteran about the killing part, honey." She darts a sympathetic glance at me as she adds, "If he wants to tell you, he'll tell you in his own time."

Pip is instantly chastened. "What's your father's name?"

"Robert Givens, Captain, United States Army. I want you to meet him while he still has most of his mind. That would be good for both of you."

Mary strokes Pip's cheek with a sad smile. Suddenly she looks at her watch. "Well, got to go. It's been a great day, you two. Thanks." She bends down to kiss Pip on the forehead. She stands up and looks at me with intent. "Enjoy your Memorial Day weekend, Mortie. Thank you for your service and for your sacrifices."

It's like an echo that has taken a week to come around. It's like I'm on stage in Act Two after having blown my lines in Act One and I now have a second chance to get an important scene just perfectly right. I want to step into her invitation and kiss her on the cheek but her *sacrifices* has stabbed me in my brain and a dozen images explode in me at once, all of them the faces of buddies who made the ultimate sacrifice. I feel unclean trying to get a little action on the basis of my supposed standing as a war hero.

"Drive safely, Mary," I say to her.

She nods and smiles. She goes to the door.

I don't follow her to the door but Pip does. I watch Mary's smooth backside walking away from me but I have no regrets this time.

"Can you come and get us when you're ready to leave?" Pip asks.

"Honey, I'm not going to the airport or anything," Mary laughs. "I'm just going to throw a few things in a suitcase. Then I'll get in my car and drive off."

"I want to see you drive off," Pip says.

"Okay. I'll knock on my way out."

Pip and I end up standing in the car courtyard and waving at Mary as she drives off, like we won't see her again for ages.

Pip says, "She's got a really sporty car for an old lady, huh?"

"Yeah," I say. "That's a pretty hot model for any age of driver."

"But Mary really isn't old, is she? Not really."

"No, not really."

I think quite suddenly and inexplicably of Mary's bosom. It's modest but it's still quite perky – or at least perky-looking in her bra. This image comes of her bra coming off and her standing there inviting me wordlessly, with a smile, to have a feel of them. Dottie laughs at that.

"She's driving too fast," Pip says fretfully as Mary rounds a corner and disappears.

Memorial Day Weekend

After seeing Mary off, Pip and I both admit that we are a little depressed in Mary's absence and we decide to cheer ourselves up by going out anyway. We decide to hit some thoroughly touristy place, sort of a mutiny against Mary's culinary snobbery. Mary has been taking us to the hip places, the cool funky out-of-the-way places, the under-the-radar delicious places known only to the locals in the know. We decide that in Mary's absence we are both essentially Bumbling Tourists in the Big City and we decide to act like it. I get us reservations at Castagnola's right on Fisherman's Wharf and we head out in a cab. Pip holds my hand all the way and I am warm. At some point I have to fight back tears as I realize that

I could have had so many moments like this with the young Charmaine, the young Melissa – even with my Dottie. *Sacrifices.* I had come back alive and unwounded but all those forgone moments of tenderness had been my war sacrifices. That hits me squarely in the gut. My buddies had left all of themselves over there. I had survived but somehow had left much of my humanity over there. How does one survive an unceasing year of combat unscathed and come home a taunt sack, seething and screaming on the inside and so mute and incapable of tenderness on the outside? How could it be that facing death and inflicting pain makes one calloused toward life and stunted in every impulse to relieve the pain and enrich the lives of others? Why didn't I come home roaring with the need to embrace, to hear, to be heard, to cry, to caress, to be touched, to soothe hurt, to make love?

If he wants to tell you, he'll tell you in his own way.

I think about something I had never thought about before, a thought I had closed out as completely as I had closed out the memory of driving my bayonet through the eyeball of that German soldier, a boy really who could not have been older than sixteen. I was only nineteen-and-a-half myself, but I felt old enough to be his grandfather. I think the ugly tragic thought that in all the years that Dottie had struggled with her drinking I had not once asked her about the source of her pain, when the pain had begun to consume her, what I might do to help. I had never even acknowledged that I knew she had a problem, even when her sad breath blew right up into my nostrils and her bleary eyes desperately begged me to show some active interest in her getting better. I had denied that part of her, and so many other parts, as I had denied so many parts of me.

"Are your parents still alive?" Pip asks over our touristy shrimp cocktails.

"Goodness, no," I puff. "My mother died when I was forty. My father died when I was sixty."

"Like Mary."

"Like Mary what?"

"Your father lived longer, like hers. Did you visit him when he was old?"

"No," I say subdued.

"Why not?"

"Because I didn't like him." *Wow!*

"Why not?"

"Are we having a night out or what?"

Unblinking brown eyes bore right through me. "Why not?" she repeats deliberately.

"Because he mistreated my mother," I snap. "Want more bread?"

"All her life he mistreated her?"

"Yes, all the time I saw them in their marriage."

"Did he hit her?"

"Look, you, this isn't fit restaurant conversation – and certainly isn't a fit topic for a nine-year-old girl."

"Did he hit her?" she asks undaunted.

I roll my eyes and sigh resignedly. "Yes. Sometimes. And that's the end of it, hear me? Enough."

Pip leans back in her chair with an adult-like deliberateness and studies me. "You should ask why I'm asking, great granddad. You shouldn't close down things when I go places I shouldn't go. You should be asking why I go to those places."

I just look at her. "What planet are you from? Tell me."

"This isn't funny, great granddad. You should ask."

"Did your dad hit your mom?" I ask cautiously.

"No, he never did."

"Did she hit him?"

"No," she says giggling. "She yelled at him like she wanted to hit him, but she never did."

"Then why do you go to that place?"

She shrugs. "I want to see where we end up if I take you there. My psychiatrist does that to me all the time. I mean, just all the freaking time. Ticks me off. It helps me though. I just wanted to try it on you. You're ticked off now, but did it help a little?"

I think about that. I think about the last time I saw my father hit my mother, the night before I left for basic training. For many nights she had dreamt of losing her only child in an artillery barrage. She had taken to her bottle to alleviate her despair. My father tolerated her secret drinking and was even resigned to my being exposed to it; but he became furious whenever she let the outside world see her "condition," as he called it. Her condition was on full display at the going-away party that our church threw for me.

"Yes," I say forthrightly to Pip. "Yeah, it has helped. Thank you." As I watch her tear off a piece of bread, so satisfied with herself, I ask, "What made you think that I needed help?"

She hesitates for just a moment, both in the buttering of her bread and with her words. She studies me sympathetically. "You talk in your sleep, great granddad. You don't yell things like mom says you used to yell, but you talk a lot."

"Last night I did?" I say shocked.

She shrugs. "Last night, and the first night I stayed with you when you were on the sofa bed. The sofa bed night I thought you were just uncomfortable and restless. But last night --"

"What did I say?"

"It was a jumble of things. You'd say, 'Eddy, watch out. We haven't cleared that area.' And then you would mumble and cry, 'Eddie! Oh, God! Eddie! Oh, God!' Then you'd quiet down for a little while and then you'd mumble, 'Don't, pop. Please don't hit her, pop. Stop it, pop, stop it.' Is Eddie one of your war buddies?"

"Yeah," I say.

"And is that your dad hitting your mom?"

"It must be, though I don't at all remember. Never have." I shake my head in wonder. "It's very strange. Sometimes I wake up screaming about my war dreams. But these domestic dreams – the dreams about being home with my parents – I have never remembered them the next morning. I don't even know how often I've dreamt them. If great grandma Dottie had not told me that I had them, I would never know that I had had them. And now you tell me." I look at Pip carefully. "Both nights I spoke out about my father?"

"Yeah. You were crying about it. You sounded like a very frightened little boy. Did he hit her hard?"

I reach out and cover her hand. "I thank you for walking me down that path," I say to her, adult-to-adult, "but I really don't want to talk any more about it tonight. About any of it. All right?"

"All right," she says earnestly.

From that point onward we talk about nothing heavy. But I feel so much lighter about myself. We have a great meal. We try to carry on a conversation in pig-Latin about her favorite subjects in school. She is absolutely fluent in pig-Latin; I struggle.

"Hattay oybay athay extnay abltay," I say haltingly. "Ehay isay terestedinay niay ouyay."

She shoots a quick urgent glance in the direction of my discreet nod. A young boy, perhaps, eleven or twelve, is staring right at her.

"Dude," she says sharply to him, "stop staring, okay? It's rude."

"Pip!" I whisper urgently, too mortified to look in the boy's direction.

"Well," she says calmly. "There's such a thing as manners. Right?"

"And there's such a thing as other people's feelings too. You have to learn to protect people a little when they reach out to you."

"He was reaching out to me? Why?"

I shake my head as I wipe the sudden sweat from my brow. "I guess I should be relieved that you are still nine in that particular way."

"In what particular way?"

"Never mind," I say, looking at the approaching waiter and desperately glad to have another human being to focus on. "Finally, our clam chowder, huh? Great."

On Saturday morning I awake to find her sitting in a chair bedside my bed.

"How long have you been there?" I say.

"An hour maybe."

"What?"

"You woke me up with your sleep-talking, so I just came in and sat down to listen to you."

"This is an invasion of my privacy, you know. I want you to stop doing this – right now."

"Not my fault. You woke me up. I just moved closer for a better listen."

"What did I say?"

"You were trying to save your buddies. Charlie and Boomer? The forest?"

I nod. "Thank you," I murmur.

"The 'fucking forest' you called it."

"That's enough," I snap.

We go down to breakfast. Without Mary there to monopolize Pip, she draws a crowd of elders who treat her like a Hollywood celebrity. They just won't let go of her. Pip takes me, and several elders in train, up to the library and gives us a one-hour seminar on the internet.

The elders are just flabbergasted to discover that they can call up some of their favorite '50's television programs on a free website. After the seminar, we all spend another hour watching two *I Love Lucy* episodes. I have to virtually shut the door in their faces to prevent them from following us into my apartment.

We go at it in *Axis and Allies* for nearly two hours and just barely make it down to lunch before the dining room closes. After delicious prime rib and mashed potatoes we go back up for another hour of war and two hours of my listening to music and cat-napping while she sketches. In early evening, we walk down to the Kabuki to take in *Indiana Jones and the Kingdom of the Crystal Skull*.

"Did you like it?" I ask Pip as the credits roll.

"It was okay," she says. "It's like a kid's carton, only it's a movie. Did you like it?"

"Yeah, very much. Because I was with you."

Sunday morning when I wake up, Pip is standing at my bedside. She's grinning.

"Was I talking in my sleep?"

"Boy, I'll say."

"About what?"

"There was some war stuff. You were calling out names."

"It was that funny?"

"No, the war stuff was intense. But the stuff after that was really funny." She waits for me to ask.

"What stuff?"

"You were going on about Mary."

I freeze. "What did I say?"

"Oh, no," she says dramatically, holding up her hands -- palms outward -- as if warding me off. "No child should ever say *that* stuff out loud."

"You're just making up stuff," I say annoyed, falling back into my pillow and looking up at the ceiling.

"I didn't make up the names you were calling different parts of Mary's body."

"What do you know? You're nine, you little Arab."

"Well, I know what –"

"What Ulrich told you, yeah."

It just shoots out of my mouth. I don't mean it to be funny, I really am annoyed. For a moment I hold my breath hoping that she is not inwardly disintegrating. In the next moment she giggles.

"Are you a dirty old man, great granddad? Is that what that means?"

"Stop it," I command. "Show some respect. Go wash your face or something."

She gets up and walks out laughing. "I'll bring you some apple juice – with ice. You probably need to cool off."

I lie back and marvel at the contradiction: the girl knows about phone sex and "cooling off" but has no idea why a strange boy would stare at her in a restaurant.

"Ulrich," I murmur to myself chuckling.

The guy had begun dusting his sister's intellect with his twelve-year-old-boy sexual wit but her hormones were still dormant.

Thank God.

I laugh out loud as I hear ice cubes tingling into glasses. I stop laughing when I remember Melissa at fifteen and Charmaine at fourteen. Suddenly I rage at my own age. Eighty-three going on eighty-four. I won't be here to watch Pip turn the corner into her dangerous adolescence. I won't be here to channel it lovingly and patiently, to explain it to her – like I didn't channel, love or explain to her mother when I was fifty-nine, or to her poor grandmother when I was thirty-eight. I jump up and hurry into the bathroom just as Pip is finishing in the kitchen. I close the door as I hear her padding toward the bedroom.

"Be out in a minute!" I shout.

I stand in front of the mirror and weep.

Over breakfast she says, "Tomorrow's Memorial Day, great granddad. We should visit a veterans' cemetery."

"I don't like veterans' cemeteries," I say.

"Why not?"

"I lost a lot of friends to war. I get reminded every night, as you know. I don't need to go out of my way in the daytime to be reminded."

"Maybe, visiting a cemetery will do you good. Maybe it will make things better for you. It makes things better for Mary's dad, right? I mean, he goes to the cemetery every time with her and he actually talks to dead buddies. Maybe all that makes him feel better about the war."

"Maybe he had an easy time in the war and can remember it without any problem. Not everyone in a uniform actually fought, you know. Veterans' cemeteries are full of men who didn't actually see any combat."

"He won a Silver Star and three Bronze Stars. You don't get those for shucking peanuts."

"How do you know he won combat medals?"

"I Googled him. Robert F. Givens of Dayton, Ohio. Captain, United States Army. There are websites that list who won what medals in which wars."

"You're kidding me."

"Nope," she says with a superior sense of satisfaction. "You'd know how to do that if you paid attention to what I'm trying to teach you."

I bite my tongue and spoon into my oatmeal. But I feel her big eyes on me.

"Morton A. Willbanks of Bloomington, Indiana," she says quietly, in a light tease. "Private at Omaha Beach, Distinguished Service Cross. Sergeant at Heurtgen Forest, Silver Sta –"

"All right, that's enough – I mean it," I snap. She hears enough hard edge in my voice and sees enough steel in my eyes to shut up instantly. In the silence I begin to feel a little guilty over being so rough on her. "I don't see a cemetery visit working that way for me," I mutter. "It's not like I haven't tried. There's one here in town, ten minutes from here. I went there once. Veterans' Day, 1987."

"And?" she says, coming forward in her chair.

"Do you know what a nervous breakdown is?"

She shakes her head.

"Well, it's not good. I walked to the summit of cemetery hill, past maybe two hundred rows of graves. When I got to the top and looked down on all of them I just broke into a thousand pieces and wailed until my ears ached. When I finished I didn't know where I was, didn't know my own name. I spent three days in the hospital."

"Were you praying before you broke down?"
"What?"
"Were you praying or were you just thinking and feeling bad?"
"What's your point?"

"Ulrich used to say that when you just think about hurtful things, you make it all about you hurting; but when you pray about things, if you pray long enough, you get around to making it about other people feeling better. And when you make it about other people feeling better, you are less scared for yourself, less worried about your own hurt."

I think about that. "You just made that up."

"Nope," she says proudly. "Ulrich."

"Did Ulrich pray a lot?"

"Yeah," she says. "We prayed together a lot. For our dad."

"Did it help him?" I ask cautiously.

"No," she says matter-of-factly. "But it helped us."

I lean across the table to her. "Why are you such a treasure? I really want to know."

She waves an adult-like dismissive hand at me. "Stop it, you," she says through a big grin.

Stop it, you.

Stop it, you.

It's Dottie. The hand thing and the big grin and the *Stop it, you* are all Dottie. In her happier and more self-confident days, my beloved. I grab Pip's hand and hang on.

"You alright, great granddad?"

"Yeah," I say.

Flags

I have the Argyll house car drive us to the cemetery's east gate rather than to the main gate. The only other time I have been here, I entered through the main gate and I hated the experience. As you walk through the main gate, you see straight ahead the lovely Spanish colonial style buildings which house administrative offices. The buildings' stucco is blindingly white and their red tile roofs are modest architectural treasures. To the immediate left, you see the large assembly area with its grassy patio for six hundred folding chairs and its permanent platform for big flags, speakers and honored guests. The lovely offices remind me that the human detritus of war is a tourist attraction which must be tidily managed, that the administration of remembrance is a bureaucratic process which has no heart or soul. The permanent assembly area reminds me that know-nothing politicians, bunker generals and portside admirals will always be in charge of remembrance and that all of the real agony, violence and bestiality of war will be carefully edited out of public memorializing.

But as you enter the Presidio cemetery from the east gate, you see straight ahead to the sloping green grass, the files of gray tombstones and the tall Eucalyptus trees which border the cemetery's far western perimeter. With every approaching step you feel yourself less worthy of the ground that awaits you and you become ever so aware that you are walking, breathing and holding the hand of a little loved one because those in the earth ahead of you ceased to do these things prematurely, or did them in their last days with less consciousness, with less pleasure, because painful wounds of body and mind never healed.

"The flags, great granddad," Pip exclaims breathlessly.

It is indeed a breathtaking sight. A small American flag flutters vigorously over every flat grave marker and in front of every upright tombstone. The dead march up the green slope with their flags in perfect order and occupy the summit of the hill near the southern perimeter of the cemetery in perfect rank and file. I won't look northward, not toward the little plain at the foot of the hill where the buildings and the assembly area are. There are regiments of holy dead in that direction too but I just can't look.

Pip and I walk to the middle of the slope, reading tombstones all the way. We turn southward to walk up the hill. We walk slowly, lingering over men who seemed to have lived exceptionally short or exceptionally long lives, studying the tombstone of every woman we encounter. Pip places a flower on every grave that intrigues her. She is out of flowers long before we reach the summit. When we get there, I have little choice but to turn around and look northward, at the full panorama of the dead.

"Is this the spot?" Pip asks.

I nod. "Pretty much."

"You feel okay now?"

"I don't know yet."

It is still what it was in November of 1987 – what it had been in October and November of 1944. The low-lying plain to the north, the slope which runs upward at steep incline toward the ridge to the south, thick and seemingly impenetrable forest bordering the eastern and western perimeters of the large glade that we are holding. The orientation is a little different but the topography is the same. The weather as well: cold, a light pelting mist just short of rain driven southward by a vigorous breeze. Hill 400, the Germans' perfect artillery-spotting perch is shrouded in mist. For that we are grateful. A Teller mine pops off in the distance and the scream tells us that another poor-slob messenger has lost his legs. Snipers in the trees now pick off every man who leaves his water-filled slit trench to void himself in the nearby grove. So we stay put and relieve ourselves in empty C-ration cans. The fecal stench is not overpowering. The smell of blood is much more pungent. Another pop, another scream. A deathly quiet settles over the glade and the surrounding forest, punctuated now and then by a whimper or a sneeze.

"Still okay, great granddad?" Pip asks.

"No," I say quietly.

"Pray, great granddad," she murmurs. "Don't think – pray."

She looks up at me meaningfully, takes three of my fingers and bows her head. I bow my head but I don't pray. I continue to think, to remember. But the pressure of her grasp steadies me and her periodic pulsating pressure seems to be her signal to me that she knows that I am not trying hard enough. I have not prayed in years – decades. Can I remember the last few times? Of course I can: the day we got Dottie's preliminary diagnosis I prayed and fasted for it to be the wrong diagnosis. Then I fasted and prayed for her full recovery, then for her partial recovery, then that she suffer less pain, then that God take her quickly. None of those prayers had been answered. Not a god-damned one.

"Great grandpa?" Pip says in a long drawn-out breath laced with censure.

I try now in a pro forma sort of way. *Dear Lord...*I start again: *Dear Lord.* I recall a spring day two weeks before the war ended. We were all being cautious because none of us wanted to be the war's last stupid casualty. A squad in the column ahead of us got ambushed. A chaplain crawled forward to administer last rites to wounded men dying in a personnel carrier. He somehow got through all the machine gunfire unscathed. As he prayed *Dear Lord* – we could see the words on his lips -- a sniper tore out his brain. *Dear Lord, why? Dear Lord, why any of it?* I burst. I stamp my feet, pounding them into the ground until my brittle knees make me stop. I tear my fingers out of Pip's grasp and start down the hill.

Out on the Town

By mid-June, we four settle into a nice little cycle of Tuesdays-through-Sundays-with-Pip. Charmaine brings Pip over especially early on Tuesday morning and pointedly stays for breakfast with the three of us so that she can get a feel for Mary. The three of *them* have a ladies' conversation about fashion and celebrity gossip. Charmaine leaves for work, making a big show of her maternal love and concern in front of Mary. On at least one of the Tuesday-through-Sunday days, Charmaine cabs over from South Beach and joins us for lunch downtown. On two of the days Pip, Mary and I go on long excursions (combining walking, cabbing-it and MUNI) to introduce Pip to the further reaches of San Francisco: the ferry excursions to Alcatraz, Angel Island and Sausalito, the museum at the Legion of Honor, the Cliff House, Lake Merced, Baker Beach on a warm day, the zoo. We get a few other things done: Pip buys more sketchbooks and pens; she "buys" me a set of earphones for my stereo; she "buys" me a Blackberry and I actually master a few features and functions – whatever -- under her merciless tutelage; we accompany Mary to a Fillmore newspaper vendor where she buys fashion magazines for Pip and a week's worth of Latin American dailies for herself; Mary takes us to her TAGS halfway house, to give Pip a sense of just how rough life can get when a girl is abandoned by both parents.

    In early-afternoon, we all generally return to the Argyll: me to two-hours of cat-napping and music-listening; Pip to two hours with her sketchbook; and Mary to whatever projects she has going in the world of Mary. In late afternoon we go to a museum exhibit or a matinee and then head out for dinner somewhere in North Beach or in the Mission. By the time we finish dinner it's easily nine o'clock and I'm exhausted. Mary goes off somewhere – I don't ask where and don't really want to know – and Pip and I return to the Argyll where I "chill out" with my music and Pip studies her fashion magazines and works in her sketchbooks.

Come Sunday noon, Charmaine BARTS in from Hayward (if she has spent the night in her own bed – I don't inquire), picks up Pip and takes her back to Hayward.

I just can't get over how quickly and smoothly fashion design replaces *Axis and Allies* as Pip's major intellectual interest. When I wake up in the morning, she is usually at the dining room table with her sketchbooks rather than at the sun window table hovering over the board. During our afternoon alone times, she sometimes draws me into an hour or two of battle but, more often than not, she returns to her art while I take a nap. When I awaken, she has filled several pages of one of her books. Her designs become more and more sophisticated but what impresses me more is how polished her draftsmanship becomes.

"Where did you learn to draw?" I say one day. I have no idea why I haven't asked the question before because her lines have always been rather fine.

"Drafting class," she says. "Mom started me in summer classes years ago."

"'Years ago?'" I laugh. "You're nine."

"Well, it seems like years ago," she says with a sudden adult-like weariness.

I can't help but caress her face. There *is* real weariness in her eyes. It slowly dissolves into that warm surrender.

"Would you like to take up drawing classes again?"

"Uhm," she says, her eyes nearly closed to my touch. "Mom says I can if she gets some pay raises on her job. We'll see."

Dandelions of Love

Late one morning, in the middle of invading Sinkiang province, Pip suddenly declares that she must go back to Chinatown. She needs "design inspiration" as to how ordinary Chinese-American kids dress during the summer when they don't have to go to school. I don't have the heart to tell her that Chinatown kids probably dress like other kids. I surely don't want her to think that I'm too lazy to get out, just because Mary isn't there to prod me. So, we take a cab to Chinatown and just walk around with our eyes open. Pip has her little sketch book in hand but she doesn't write or draw in it. After an hour or so we have a huge lunch in this grimy little place that Pip chooses because it's got lots of teenage patrons. I've got to admit it: it's the best Chinese food I've ever had – nothing like P. F. Chang's.

I want to take a cab back to the Argyll because I'm just stuffed and crave an afternoon nap. But Pip wants to ride the 30 Stockton because she wants to see more of her ordinary Chinese. We're standing on a corner waiting for the bus which is taking its time in getting there. She notices a bunch of dandelion blossoms growing in a small vacant lot bordering the sidewalk. She slips away from me and begins picking them. She picks three or four of them, bunches them together and blows vigorously. Dozens of white parasols shoot up into the air and float lazily to earth. She watches their descent with what strikes me as sad thoughtfulness. She repeats her game several times. I walk over to her and ask,

"What are you thinking about when you do that?"

She smiles wanly at me. "You don't want to know."

"Yeah, I do."

"It's war stuff, great granddad. I know you've had enough of that for the day. That's why I got us out into the sunshine."

"I can take it."

"Okay," she says carefully. "That's the Eighty-Second Airborne dropping out over

Sainte-Mere-Eglise on D-Day. That's what Ulrich used to say every time we did dandelions."

She has pronounced *Sainte-Mere-Eglise* like a serious French student.

"Do you know French?"

She shrugs. "A little. Mom used to have us in French immersion after-school care."

"In Mill Valley," I confirm.

She nods. "I learned a little French but Ulrich was getting really good. Sometimes when we played Axis and Allies and we fought over France, he'd start talking all this French trying to distract me. Half of it, I think, was bullshit, but a lot of it was real."

She's been gathering another handful of dandelions as she says this. Now she blows vigorously and the air in front of us fills with a battalion of descending paratroopers.

"And there's the Hundred First Airborne dropping over Carentan," she says in a distant tone, the *Carentan* nearly perfect.

I stoop, with effort, and pluck four dandelion stalks. I draw a big breath and blow hard.

"Wow!" Pip exclaims. "You've got some lungs!"

We watch my parasols float to earth.

"What are *you* thinking now?" she asks.

I wasn't thinking of anything in particular when I blew; but now that she has asked, my mind goes instantly to Ulrich. So I lie a little. "I was thinking of Ulrich," I say.

She looks up at me rather than at the last of the parasols. "What about him?"

"I was thinking these aren't paratroopers. These are little pieces of Ulrich's spirit and we're spreading them out all over the world. A lot of them will blossom."

For a long moment I think I've hurt her with my stupid attempt to say something profound. But she bends down and very deliberately picks the last dandelion in the vacant lot. She hands it to me with a formality that lets me know that this is now a ceremony. "Do it again," she says quietly. "Really hard this time. Blow'em up into the air above our heads."

I do as she says. We watch the parasols descend. She watches some catch on my hair and shoulders and I watch some catch on hers. Most fall between us, fluttering to earth in quivering little spirals. Neither of us speaks. When the last parasol settles Pip just looks at me.

The bus arrives soon thereafter. We get on and sit down. As the bus pulls away from the curb, Pip looks back at the vacant lot, and keeps looking back at it until it is out of sight. When she turns back to me I smile at her. She manages a faint little smile. I raise a hand to pick off the dandelion blossoms which still cling to her.

"No, don't," she commands quietly, with a touch of sadness.

I caress her cheek but otherwise leave her alone. We ride in silence for blocks. At no time does she seem to observe her Chinese-American kids who now boisterously fill the bus.

"Can you grow dandelions in a pot?" she suddenly asks.

"I don't think so," I say. "I think that you have to get out and just enjoy them where you find them."

"Yeah," Pip says. "That's…"

She doesn't finish her thought. And I don't press. We ride in silence for blocks.

"I think that you are an incredibly brave girl," I finally say.

She frowns at me. "Me? Why?"

"You face Ulrich's loss with such courage, honey."

"Why is it so brave to live with a hole in your heart when there is nothing you can do about it?"

I've got nothing to say to that.

She says, "Are you brave for living without great grandma Dottie?"

"No. I don't feel very brave anyway."

"There," she says with finality.

That shuts me up for a long while. More blocks. She continually looks out the window, denying her face to me. I think she's tired of me, of my silly wisdom and my hollow encouragement. I'm content to observe our fellow passengers. But she turns her face to me again. Her eyes are moist and her mouth is a tight little knit of tension.

"Did you mean what you said when we first met? That I make Ulrich live in your heart?"

"Yes, I so meant exactly that, honey. Not just in me. You make him live in the world every time you talk about him to anyone who is listening to you. Every time you tell someone what a good brother he was, he becomes a good person to that someone. Every time you tell someone how much you still love him, people think to themselves, *Wow*, and it makes them love the people in their own lives a little more. Not a whole lot more -- just a little more. But it doesn't take much love to make a big difference in someone's life. It's so powerful."

She cocks her head to one side and gives me this skeptical squint – just like her mother used to do. In that moment I pray to God that she doesn't ruin the moment by telling me, *You are so full of shit, great granddad.* Instead she says:

"Like garlic."

"What?"

"Love is like garlic sort of. It doesn't take a lot to make a big difference in the taste of something. And it lingers."

"Yeah," I say in wonder. "Like garlic." Involuntarily my hand reaches up and takes hold of all of her little chin and jaw. "Do you have any idea what a marvel you are?"

"What's a marvel?"

"Something wonderful. Something very special."

She shrugs. She looks at me with this resigned vulnerable look that brings tears to my eyes. She wipes away the first tear that rolls. She picks a parasol from my sleeve and puts it in her hair.

Alcohol and History

The next night, the three of us are enjoying a late-night meal in a Peruvian restaurant on Fillmore. Mary starts making noises about not wanting to let go of Pip and it being too early for me to push Pip into bedtime retirement.

"Early?" I say laughing. "It's nearly nine thirty."

"I know, I know," Mary says.

"I can tell you now," I say. "At least two people at this table qualify for a long night's sleep on age alone." I look leeringly at Mary. "How old are you again?"

I mean it to be funny, my second sad attempt at humor in years. But Mary is anxious, fidgety, and she's been like that all evening. I've never seen her like that. I must look overlong because she holds my eye and says, "Long day with my TAGS. I was on the phone for three hours with this ten-year-old girl who came within heartbeats of blowing her brains out. I was in my automatic rescue mode when I was on the phone with her. But now…I'm just now really thinking about it and I…" She looks at Pip. She reaches across the table and takes Pip's hand. "Sorry, honey, you didn't need to hear all that. But I want you to know why I treasure you so much right now, why I love you so much and don't want to let you go tonight."

Pip gets out of her chair, comes around to Mary's side of the table and gives her a big hug. Mary holds on to her with a desperate passion. As they disengage Mary pulls Pip's head into her and gives her a big wet kiss on the cheek. Pip fixes me with these moist beseeching eyes.

"We can stay out a little later tonight, can't we, great granddad?"

"Just let me take her to this great new boutique on Sacramento Street," Mary pleads. "It's their grand opening tonight. The owner is Argentinean and won't close up until eleven or so."

"She can't go anywhere without me," I say. "Charmaine's strictest orders."

"Then come with us," they both plead in nearly perfect unison.

"Come on, great granddad," Pip insists. "You don't have to move much – the cab will do all the work."

But I'm not only stuffed and tired. My stomach has begun to act up. I just want Pepto Bismol, a little Scarlatti and my bed.

"Another time," I say.

Pip is deeply disappointed. God, how I've spoiled her in so little time. Mary looks at me like I'm an old fart bag. I don't care so much about that but the indulgent elder in me overwhelms my good sense.

"Okay, all right," I say. "You two go on without me. But door-to-door in a cab -- and, Pip, do *not* answer your mother's phone calls until you're back at my place. Understood?"

"Yes, sir!" Pip nearly shouts as she emphatically salutes me.

"And don't stay out longer than an hour and a half. I'm timing you."

They both nod gratefully.

I see them off in a cab and then climb into a cab of my own. As soon as I settle in, I begin to fret over my decision. How could I do this to Charmaine? How could I have put myself in this position? Jesus, if Charmaine somehow finds us out…

I recall Charmaine's early teenage years when I'd catch her in a lie or in a broken commitment not to drink or fornicate. She would cover her tracks so brilliantly but I would catch her anyway. Every time I caught her.

"You're fucking spying on me!" she would scream.

Most times I would smile grimly and say, "No, I'm not spying, Charmaine. This is your karma. It is the fate of a dishonest person to be found out. Always. Get used to it."

Some time in her late-teenage years, Charmaine stopped confronting me directly and gainsaying me right off the bat. She discovered the tactic which had been her mother's from day one of her own wild adolescent career. Charmaine began sweetly agreeing with everything I said. She began forthrightly committing to some rule or deadline or curfew that I would impose. Then she would break the living hell out of whatever commitment she had made and smile sweetly through my volcanic disappointment in her. She would just wait for me to stomp off in frustration and then proceed merrily along with her outrageous life.

I open my apartment door and cross my threshold feeling incredibly guilty that I am crossing it alone. I have in the pit of my stomach an aching feeling unrelated to the Peruvian food that is sloshing around in there. I take my

Pepto Bismol, put on some Scarlatti and settle into my easy chair to wait. Every two or three minutes I look at my watch. I kick myself: both Mary and Pip have cell phones. Why aren't their numbers in my Blackberry? Why have I put myself in the position of not being able to call them and tell them that I have changed my mind, that I want them to get their behinds home right now?

An hour passes. Two. It's nearly midnight! I can't believe that Mary is this irresponsible. I put on some Schumann to calm me. Halfway through his piano concerto I hear a knock. I'm there quickly, opening the door to the two of them.

"Granddad!" Pip exclaims.

"Sorry, Mortie," Mary says just as quickly. "I know you're upset. My fault. The proprietress of the boutique just fell in love with Pip. We stayed in her shop talking even after she closed and then she took us to her home to talk some more."

"And you couldn't have called," I mutter.

"She was *so* interesting, great granddad! You can't imagine! She sold her first designs in Buenos Aires when she was *seven*! And she knows all about the Falklands War!"

They're still standing outside the door, like I have to invite them in.

"Come in," I grumble. "Why are you standing out there?"

They file past me and that is when I smell the brandy on Mary. For some reason, my eyes go straight to Pip. She now strikes me as being a little glass-eyed. I advance on her, stoop down and inhale.

"What the hell, Mary?" I say. "You let her drink?"

"Oh, relax. She had a couple of sips of peach brandy."

"A lot of sips!" Pip pipes up.

"What the hell are you doing?" I scream at Mary. "She's nine, for God's sakes! What in hell were you thinking?"

They are both stunned to paralysis by the sudden volume and intensity of my distress.

"Mortie, peach brandy, all right?"

"I don't give a damn! It's AL-CO-HOL! AND SHE'S NINE!"

"I'm sorry –"

"The whole damned world is full of sorry, Mary! THE WHOLE FUCK-ING WORLD IS FULL of SORRY! How many of your TAGS have booze problems, huh? How many of their parents? WHY ARE THERE HALFWAY HOUSES IN THE FIRST PLACE, MARY? Ever thought about that?" I grab her by her upper arms and scream, "What the FUCK-ING HELL WERE YOU THINKING!"

I feel my heart coming out of my chest. That's the only reason I stop yelling, the only reason I retreat from Mary's face which I now realize I've pushed my own face right up into. It is only when I stumble back that I look at Pip, who is staring at me with those big doe eyes. Her mouth is trembling, her whole body quaking like she's freezing.

"I should go," Mary says quietly, also looking at Pip now.

"Yeah, you should," I snap between gasps for air.

But Mary has not retreated one step. "I am so sorry." She turns to Pip. "I'm sorry, honey."

"Call my mama," Pips says as she breaks down into tears. "I want my mama! I want to go home!"

"It's best, Mortie," Mary says.

"You have no idea what's 'best' for her. Just get out."

Mary looks sadly at me, at Pip. She studies my eyes as she says cautiously, "We've both messed up a little here, Mortie. I think she could use a break from both of us." She says to Pip as she keeps a cautious eye on me: "Got your phone?"

Pip nods, her eyes still fixed in terror on me.

"Call your mom, honey."

Pip runs into the bedroom and slams the door. My legs are about to give out. I collapse into a chair. After a few more furious beats of my heart, I hear:

"Mama! Mama, come and get me! No, now! NOW!"

Oh, God, what have I done? What is wrong with me? I feel a vice closing on my heart. I can't breathe. My head aches with a ferocity that increases with my every heartbeat.

"Mortie?" Mary calls out with tentative worry. "Mortie?" she repeats.

I hear my name a third time, but from a great distance, and a fourth time as a whisper. Then blackness.

Alone with History

It is late. I stand in the entry way staring at the front door. The window panels which flank the door are dark and water-streaked. Over the sound of pelting rain I hear a car engine outside. I have an urge to run out but I fight the urge. I will something good to happen but I have no idea what. The door finally opens. Charmaine, in heels much too high and a skirt far too short, floats in on the air chariot of her first drunk.

The first one that Dottie and I have been exposed to anyway.

Dottie rushes to Charmaine and tearfully throws arms around her. I stand back trying to tamp down the heat building in my brain.

My windows are open. An urgent siren wafts up to me from the world outside. Charmaine is gone now. And Pip. But my brain is still hot. I wonder how far back it goes: the dream, or the foggy recollection in my semi-comatose state, or whatever it was. Is all of Pip part of the dream? Did I conjure all of her up? Does Charmaine even have a daughter? I rise from my bed and wander through my other rooms. I see no evidence of a little girl ever having been present. Her ice cream bowl is not in the kitchen sink; her sketchbooks are not on the dining room table; her pink suitcase is not discreetly tucked behind the living room sofa; worst, the *Axis and Allies* board and box are not on the sun window table. All of it a dream? Or has Charmaine thoroughly packed up everything so that she will never have to call me and ask *Did we leave…?*, so that she will never have to speak to me ever again.

I step on something, something little but hard in the carpet. I turn on brighter lights to see what it is. An infantryman, a German one. I am relieved: not a dream then. But I am devastated: *I had her in my life, I did, and I blew it*. I belatedly recall that I have blown Mary too. I know for sure that she is gone forever. She hadn't wasted one tear on me as I beat her down with my ugly fury. Just that look of disappointment in me, like I was an adopted pound dog who had messed the carpet. All her concern had been for Pip.

I go back to the bedroom and lie down. I attempt a chronological review of everything, to separate history from dream from conjured images. I try to be systematic about it, putting *real* in one mental tray, *dream* in one, *conjured* in another. I try so many times to put my rage in the dream tray. I admit to being a little annoyed. Perhaps I was angry, but justifiably so. Perhaps I raised my voice a little too much. But I couldn't really have…

It nearly works. But every time I think I'm close to some sort of closure that works to my advantage, Pip's terrified face rises up. Or Mary's disappointed face. Oh, God, the utterly disgusted face of Charmaine when she finally arrives to take Pip away. And then I remember the real chronology of things: Pip had not waited in my place for her mother to come and collect her. She had gone off with Mary to Mary's place to wait. Because Mary had insisted on that and Pip had convinced her mother over the phone that she also wanted that, felt safer with that. Because I was a crazy angry old man and I couldn't be trusted not to go off again.

Not tonight, dear. She's drunk. It's not a good time to confront her. She can't process things. Let her sleep it off and we'll have a reasonable family discussion in the morning. Dottie's breath smells of the scotches and brandies as she says this. Beautiful Dottie: even sauced, her loving patience with Charmaine breaks through every layer of her own pain.

But the next morning, the family discussion turns ever so quickly into a screaming war. Charmaine and I practically nose to nose, exhausted Dottie in between trying her best. I say horrible things, use ugly words. The closest I come to saying anything loving and paternal is, *You'll wake up one morning with syphilis in your mouth and you won't remember where it came from.*

I roll to my bed stand to call Charmaine, to make sure that she and Pip have arrived home safely, to see just how much damage I have done to Pip's psyche. Beside my telephone on my bed stand is a cell phone. I remember: it's a Blackberry, it's mine, Pip. I am pleased that I can dial Charmaine's number with those tiny buttons.

"Yes?" Charmaine says with some hostility.

"I am so sorry," I say. "I've messed up so badly."

"Have you any idea how fragile Pip is – how fragile she was when she came to you? How could you shout at her? Didn't you get enough of that with me?"

"I didn't shout at her," I say desperately. "I was shouting at Mary."

"You think that's a big distinction to Pip right now?"

"What can I do to make it up to her?"

"And you *swore* at her?"

"Not at her –"

"At her, in front of her – it doesn't matter! When are you going to get it? Your anger destroys! It just kills every living thing!"

"I am so sorry."

"You used to take the skin off my face because I drank with my friends but it's all right for your friend to get my daughter drunk? How does that work? Tell me."

"I've got nothing to say for myself," I manage to get out. "I've just got nothing. I am so sorry."

"Really," she says flatly.

"What are you going to do now?"

"About what?"

"Day care for Pip."

Charmaine laughs bitterly. "Well, that's certainly none of your worry now, is it? Gotta go."

She clicks off.

I lie inertly on my bed for uncounted hours, until my bladder threatens to burst. I get up and take care of business, wash my face. I can't stand to look at my image in the mirror and I don't. I go sit in my sun window and watch the city come to life at dawn. I decide that I will sit there until I die, remain utterly inert lest I do more damage in the world before I expire.

My Blackberry goes off in the bedroom. It plays that silly little melody that Pip loaded into it. I am not at all inclined to answer it until I remember that only two people in the world have my cell phone number: Charmaine and Pip, and Charmaine is done with me in this lifetime. I hurry into the bedroom. Pip's name appears on caller ID.

"Hello, honey!" I virtually yell.

"Hello, great granddad," she says in a low conspiratorial voice. "How are you feeling?"

"Pretty lousy. I'm so sorry, honey. Please forgive me."

"Forgiven," she says offhandedly. "But I don't need to do that so much. I wasn't the one you attacked. Have you apologized to Mary?"

"No."

"What are you waiting for? You owe her big time."

"Well, it's early in the morning. I haven't really thought about apologizing."

"Haven't *thought* about apologizing?"

"It's not like that," I say desperately. "I'm just too ashamed to think clearly, I guess."

"Don't wait, great granddad. It only gets harder with time. Ulrich used to say that an owed apology is like curdled milk in your stomach. You try to tell yourself that you can keep it down and digest it, but eventually it's going to make you sick and you're going to have to throw it up anyway. So you might as well throw it up now and save yourself some trouble."

"You are so right, honey. Ulrich was so wise. Did he need to apologize to you a lot?"

"Sometimes," she says, suddenly subdued. "Sometimes he'd lose his temper and say hurtful things. He always made it good though. I'd just wait for him to make it good and he always did. You need to make it good with Mary, great granddad. We were a great team, the three of us. You tore a big hole in us."

My heart implodes. "Oh, honey," is all I can say. I begin to disintegrate.

"Stay with me here, great granddad. Get a grip, okay?"

"Okay," I say, snuffling.

"Mom's making these whacked-out daycare plans for me. I mean *whacked*. She's desperate, she's not thinking clearly. You've got to step up to the plate, show her that you can be trusted again. I mean, *like now*."

"I don't see me convincing her, honey. I let you go out with a stranger. I gave your mom my guarantee that I wouldn't, and I broke that guarantee. That got you drunk."

"I was *not* drunk," she says emphatically. "Some older people need to lighten up here. Anyway, mom and Mary are all cool about that now. They had a really long talk last night."

"In Mary's room?"

"No, on the drive home. Mary drove mom and me home last night."

"To Hayward?" I say, shocked.

"Yeah. Mary insisted on it. She saw how completely exhausted mom was and just wouldn't let her out the door until mom agreed to let her drive us home. You should have seen her. I mean, she blocked her door and wouldn't let mom and me out."

"So your mom's car is still here at the Argyll?"

"Yeah. She parked it in the garage there. This morning she's got to BART-it into San Francisco and go get it. So when she shows up there, you make sure you see her. She doesn't want to talk to you and she'd just as soon get her car and leave without seeing you, but you have *got* to talk to her, great granddad. Clean it up."

"How will your mother –"

"Oh, gotta go!" Pip suddenly whispers with great urgency. "Mom's alarm clock just went off – I'm not supposed to be speaking to you – bye!"

She clicks off. I stand there staring at the Blackberry, savoring the dead air. I thank God for Pip. For Ulrich. I resolve that I will never again do anything to threaten their places in my life.

Mary.

I suddenly feel like total shit. I sink into the bed and start the self-flagellation. A voice starts droning in my inner ear, a very distant voice. I recognize it and I laugh. It is Mrs. Lucy Culver, my high school English teacher. Seven decades ago she said something that has obviously stuck because I recite aloud now: Whatever is worth saying to another human being is worth rehearsing.

My lungs, my muscles and my morale all suddenly inflate. I do an old man's version of bounding off the bed. I go into the bathroom and clean myself up. I shave, all the time rehearsing for Mary.

Mary in a Robe

"Mortie?" Mary says incredulously, sleep-leaden, from the other side of her door. She has obviously looked through her peep hole.

"It's me, Mary."

She opens the door. She smiles at me squinting. My eyes drop down the front of her. She's got on a kimono and the silk clings to her.

"I've got to talk to you, Mary. Normally I wouldn't disturb you so early, but I suspect that you're alone because I know you've been playing chauffeur all night."

"She called you, huh?" she says smiling and blinking. "Come in."

I enter. She doesn't leave me much clearance to pass. I brush against her, eyeing her.

I like the sleepy look. I imagine waking up to it, to what's under the kimono. But I'm there to save my future with my great granddaughter, and that's what I'm thinking about for the most part.

"How are you feeling?" she asks.

"I'm fine."

I suddenly remember the obvious: someone else summoned the house nurse after my intemperate breakdown.

"Thank you for summoning Nurse Jane," I say humbly.

"Did she help?"

"She took my blood pressure – which was too high – and gave me a sedative. It all worked out. I'm here to apologize to you, Mary. I am so very stupid and I am so very sorry. I really must be out of my mind to snap off at the root with the only friend I have in this world. I don't say what I'm about to say as an excuse – please don't take it that way. But you have a right to know what drove my insane behavior last night. You see, all the significant females in my life have abused alcohol. Every single one that I lived with and cared for abused the hell out of it. My wife; my daughter until she graduated to drugs; my grand daughter Charmaine; even my mother. In every case, I think, having to live with me contributed to the problem."

"Oh, Mortie."

"No, it's true. Thank God, Charmaine has made a nice recovery in life. But the others... Anyway, I smelled Pip's breath and all of that just exploded in me. The rage, the fear, the violent resolve not to let it happen again. But you didn't deserve any of that, not one second of it. Forgive me. Please."

Mary pulls her kimono a little more tightly around her and brings one hand up to my cheek.

"Thank you, Mortie. I forgive you."

"Thank you," I say, just managing to keep my voice steady. Her touch is so warm. I congratulate myself for having had the foresight to shave.

"I want you to know something," Mary says. "I told all of this to Charmaine last night but I want you to hear it too. I wasn't being some careless drunk when I shared alcohol with Pip. I was introducing her to alcohol in a measured and responsible way, trying to lay the groundwork for her to enjoy alcohol throughout her life in a measured and responsible way. I see it in your eyes. 'At *nine* years old?' you're thinking. And I say, 'Yes.' I say that I see them that young at the center every single week, as hollowed-eyed as their mothers. We – Pip and I – had a little talk about moderate drinking and self-regard as we talked about brandies and liqueurs. Now, I know it wasn't my place to do all that. I know that. I know it was particularly stupid to do it in her mother's absence and without her mother's permission. I just got carried away because I'm so much in love with Pip and I want to add my two cents of influence to her life. And after hearing Charmaine's jackass comment on alcohol that night in Union Square, I just felt a need to impart some balance to the situation. I know I've got no right to think about Charmaine in those terms – I admitted that to her last night. And after my confession she of course got very angry. But she went on to explain to me why she felt as she did." Mary adds cautiously, "She talked a little about her childhood."

"About the way I treated her?"

"Yes, that too, but more about her grandma Dottie…about her drinking. I think you two are on the same page, in so many ways. Here I go again, swimming out of my depth, but I think that it's past time you two had a real conversation."

"What did she say about Dottie?"

Mary shakes her head. "You two talk about that. I just want to complete what's appropriate for me to complete. You asked me last night if I was aware of why we need shelters and halfway houses in the first place. Let me tell you, Mortie, I know better than most. It's that bitter knowledge that drives me to educate young girls on drinking whenever I get the chance. If a girl speaks any of the languages I speak, we talk, and then we talk some more. All that being said, I'm very sorry that I stepped out of bounds with you and Charmaine. I really am. Please, forgive me."

"That's okay," I hear myself say. "I very much want you to have influence over Pip, Mary. She's already so much more healed, so much more whole, because of you. You're a great influence to have in one's life."

Silence. She looks at me like I'm something special. I can't describe her look otherwise, I can't process it intellectually. I just savor it. Very deliberately she rewraps her kimono. For just an instant I see flesh. Suddenly I want her so much that I can taste her.

"Thanks, Mortie," she finally says.

The silence has stretched out so long that I have forgotten why she's thanking me.

"That's such a sweet thing to say," she says humbly. "That's a gift to me."

Her tone is so intimate, so immediate. Stupid me, I can't be comfortable in the moment. I've got to talk, to dial back the intensity of things by saying something stupid.

"Anyway," I say, "who am I to be a gatekeeper of influence? I've never really been equipped to have any sort of influence over a young life, not even as a young father, not even as a middle-aged one. Thank God I'm just a great grandfather to Pip. I've just got enough to be a babysitter. Now that I've been forced to step back from things, I can say that I don't want any part of the job that Charmaine has before her."

Another silence now, one with a less warming texture. Mary's look is now laced with a slight grimace.

"I think you've got the job anyway," Mary says solemnly. "And I think you should be honored to have it." When I fail to come back, she adds: "Pip is changing at a million miles an hour. Someone's got to keep pace with that change. Someone's got to channel it, explain it to her when she's confused by it. Her mother is too busy trying to make ends meet. She goes to work exhausted – I see it in her eyes when she has breakfast with us. I saw it in her eyes last night, and it wasn't just the drive in from Hayward after a long day's work. It's exhaustion to the bone marrow. I've been a single mom. I've been there with my own nine-year-old. Charmaine has very little to give Pip at the end of a day, no matter how much she wants to give more. She needs you as much as Pip does, Mortie. You've got to pick up your mitt. You've got to dust it off and get back in the game."

"Thanks for the pep talk," I say neutrally.

"Do I detect a hint of self pity there?"

"Maybe," I say defensively.

"Have those been the twin poles in the life of Morton Arthur Willbanks?" she asks undaunted. "Rage and self-pity?"

She brings a hand up to my face again. She starts to say more but changes her mind. She settles for a smile. I don't like that smile. It's patient, it's indulgent, it's the smile of a developed human being shepherding a less-developed human being toward completeness. Completeness. I'll show her completeness. I grab the back of her head and pull it into me. I kiss her right on the lips and I tear at the kimono until it surrenders the swell of her left breast. I kiss her there too. I stab at her mouth again. She does not tense up, she does not resist, she is not impressed. She just looks at me like we're in the middle of a casual conversation and she's waiting for me to complete a sentence. I release her and march quickly to the door. I rip open the door and leave without looking back.

I wish I could say it was a Clark Gable sort of exit: make my emphatic point on the girl's mouth and march out leaving her breathless. The truth is, I looked into Mary's eyes and I realized that I would have to work for my possibilities with her. I saw that all her come-ons were just invitations to rise to some minimum level of worthiness. I saw all that and I just got damned scared. If my bladder hadn't been empty, I would have wet myself.

Mortie, I sneer to myself as I walk down the hall refusing to look back at her. I'm no Mortie. I'm Morton A. Willbanks, and apparently I am not only dick-less, I am apparently clue-less.

Nice

But I still have hopes of being a wonderful great grandfather and I leave Mary's place resolved to fight for that. I hurry down to the lobby. It's nearly six-thirty in the morning and I don't want to miss Charmaine when she comes in. I tell the receptionist that I might fall asleep in a lobby chair in the next few minutes but I am to be awakened as soon as my granddaughter arrives, and that under no circumstances is she to be allowed to collect her car from the Argyll garage until she has spoken to me.

    I settle into a lobby easy chair and fall asleep. I awake when Charmaine shakes me awake. Her big doe eyes fill up my sleep-fogged vision and for a moment I think I am dreaming of Pip as a grown woman.

"You wanted to see me?" she says.

I am instantly alert. "To apologize. I am sorry that I betrayed your trust, that I added to your burdens."

She is unmoved. "It's all right," she says neutrally. "It worked out in a way. I got to know Mary a little better, to get over what she did."

"She's such a fine woman."

"I don't know about all that – I mean, I really don't. I know she's generous and caring – no doubt about that. Like you are. But generosity and caring don't keep a young girl safe. That's all I need right now for Pip: safety. I don't need her in a new outfit every other day, I don't need fireworks going off in her intellectual world every day. I just need her safe. I need not to have to worry about her while I'm working twelve hours a day."

"She is safe, Charmaine."

"I'm not going to argue it now, understand? It's over. Pip is safe now and we're moving on."

"Moving on with what childcare for Pip?"

"I have to say it again? Not your concern."

"Who's she with today? I don't want strangers looking after her!"

She grimaces at my temper – *my temper*. She turns from me and starts toward the lobby elevator that will take her down to the basement garage. I look at her back, her tired back, and I see my life evaporating – and in that moment, more than all my moments with Pip, I cherish my own life and am afraid for it.

"I am so sorry I failed you!" I cry out. She does not even break her stride. "I am so sorry I failed your mother!" I break down. I sob. She stands there looking at her feet until the elevator comes. I can't get my legs to move toward her. The elevator comes. She gets on. The doors close.

Sweet Silence

I sit in that chair in the lobby for hours. I've got no place to be, nothing I want to do. A dozen Argyll staffers come to me and ask if I'm all right. The reception desk worker finally calls Mary and asks her to come down and check on me. Overhearing that phone conversation from the receptionist's end embarrasses me and galvanizes me into getting up. I go back up to my place before Mary can come down. I don't want to see her. I don't want to see anyone ever again except for Pip. I remember that I've slept perhaps five hours in the last thirty. I take my blood pressure and go to bed.

I look at my Blackberry on the bed stand. Why didn't I get Pip's number? Why didn't she load it into my phone when we bought it? There is a knock at my door. A second louder knock, Mary's knock.

"Mortie?"

I just lie there. No need to move, even for her. My life is over. A few minutes later my land line rings. I suspect it's Mary trying again. Still no need. I reach for it only when I realize that I've got to get up anyway for my bladder's sake. By then the phone has stopped ringing. I go to the bathroom and take care of business. I go back to bed and lie there playing a game with myself: If I really believe my life to be over, would I bother to get up to pee? Wouldn't I just lie here and pee on myself, and keep peeing on myself until I died? I laugh. The twin poles of Morton Arthur Willbanks: rage and self-pity.

My land line rings. I awake to a semi-dark room. I've slept the day away. I listen to the phone ringing, testing my earlier resolve to just lie there until death comes. I feel somewhat refreshed and convince myself that much of my earlier despair was simple exhaustion. I think about Charmaine's long days and my heart swells with admiration for her.

While I'm in the bathroom, my Blackberry rings. I finish my business quickly, but by the time I get to the phone it has stopped ringing and the caller ID screen is blank. Thank God: I suddenly remember that I was paying attention when Pip was showing my how to access my phone log. I can get Pip's number!

My heart stops. It's Charmaine, not Pip. But I stare slack-mouth at the screen.

Charmaine Willbanks.

At some point in time she had jettisoned "Carpenter," her married name, and returned to her mother's maiden name. To *my* name.

"Thank you for returning my call," Charmaine says solemnly.

"Sure," I say with my heart in my throat.

"Just thought you'd like to know. Pip stepped on the bathroom scale this evening. She's gained eight pounds since she first came to you."

"That's great."

"Yeah. She had been steadily losing weight since…since Ulrich died, so this is quite an achievement. She gives you all the credit. You and Mary."

"Yeah, we've had some great meals. The Argyll food is great, as you know, and we've been porking it up in some pretty good restaurants."

I decide that I'm babbling. I shut up. A long silence, except I think I hear Pip's faint voice in the background.

"Anyway," Charmaine says, straining to sound casual, "Pip promises me that she will definitely go on a hunger strike until I agree to let her come back to the Argyll. She didn't eat all day today. She won't touch her dinner."

"Well, put her on the phone. I'll set her straight."

"No, it's not that. I gave in. I'm calling to tell you that I agreed. That is, if you're still willing."

"Still…*willing?* Oh, God, this saves my life, Charmaine. Thank you."

"Well, there's another reason. Pip finally showed me her sketchbooks. She finally opened up to me about how you and Mary are inspiring her. I had to unlock her suitcase to find out about these sketchbooks. That did not thrill me."

Charmaine sounds a little hurt, betrayed.

"She wasn't closing you out," I say quickly. "She said several times that she didn't want to bring more distraction into your life. She's very sensitive to how hard you work and how little energy you have for new complications."

"But you should have told me."

"She made me promise not to. Believe it or not, I can keep a promise now and then."

I chuckle out of sheer nervousness. To my surprise Charmaine laughs a truncated little laugh. More silence.

"I need to know Mary better," she says. "I should get to know the woman who is taking over my daughter's life."

I rush to defend Mary against that one but Charmaine quickly says:

"So I want you to bring her to a lunch or early dinner at my place this Sunday. Nothing fancy – nothing like the three of you have been eating."

"Why don't we come out there and take you out to dinner?" I say, thrilled. "Don't want you slaving over a stove on your day off."

"No, I want face time with her on my own turf, humble though it may be. Not in the Argyll dining room, not in a fancy restaurant, not in her room, not in her car. Can you come or not?"

I freeze. Why the hell am I making such ambitious plans? I've never asked Mary to go any place with me. I've never had to – there's always been Pip to propel us.

"I'll have to check with Mary," I say a little embarrassed. "She's an incredibly busy woman."

"Ah, but not too busy to monopolize my daughter three or four days a week." She says this with shameless jealousy. She sighs with some disgust. "Well, check with her and get back to me. And by the way, my boss will be at the dinner too. His name is Paul, just in case anyone there is interested in him as a human being."

"I recall his name from our introduction."

"It's about time Pip got used to seeing him around me – yeah, he's my boyfriend and I'm not ashamed of it."

"When you're willing to pull him out into the light with a smile on your face, there's no reason why you should be, honey."

There is silence at her end. Then:

"That makes a lot of sense. That's nice of you to say."

Nice. On her lips. I remember her *nices*. I remember her last one with me: she's twelve and she's holding my hand and I've just bought her an ice cream after first telling her that she should save her appetite for Dottie's pot roast.

"You can't tell her we had ice cream," I warn. "And you can't spill any of that on your dress. She will know."

Charmaine winks at me. "This is fun," she says, licking the ice cream. Her eyes light up like birthday candles when I break down and get an ice cream of my own. "This is nice," she says giggling. "This is so nice, granddad."

"Thank you, granddad," Charmaine says, but with a little more emotion. "I'm going to tell Paul what you said. That will give him quite a bit of encouragement."

"That's good, honey."

"This could actually be a lot of fun on Sunday. Oh, speaking of Sundays, we'll go back to her being with you just Tuesday-through-Friday. I miss her too much."

"Okay," I say readily.

"Talk to Mary about a week from Sunday. Get back to me soon. Okay?"

"All right," I say – and out of nowhere I blurt out: "Thank you, honey."

She is taken aback. "For what?" she asks.

"For Pip. For giving me a second chance."

She knows the deeper agenda – I sense it.

"You've got nothing to apologize for," she says with a sudden flatness. But I hear the bitterness behind the flatness. "Get back to me," she says, and hangs up.

Question is...

"She wants to show herself off in the most favorable light," I say to Mary. "And to show Pip that mom is still in control of things despite this glamorous charismatic older woman coming out of nowhere to dazzle everybody."

Mary glows. She has never struck me as the kind of woman who is a sucker for a backhand compliment.

"And," I add, "I don't think that she ever recovered from us discovering her in Union Square that night."

"She's got nothing to be ashamed of," Mary says suddenly annoyed, as if she herself has been challenged in some way. "She's a woman in full charge of her own life."

Anger swells in her. I suspect that she is reliving some episode with a close-minded sexual hypocrite in her own past.

"Well," I say, "I don't know whom she's more anxious to impress: you or Pip."

"Don't judge it, Mortie. Aside from her owing nobody anything, it's a good thing either way. So, are you inviting me or not?"

"Sorry. I didn't make that clear?"

"No. So far, you've been briefing me on the contours of your domestic landscape. What Charmaine would like from me. How Pip would enjoy having me there. How it'll ease Charmaine's boss into Pip's life. I haven't exactly heard my place in all this from *your* point of view."

"I don't want you to feel any pressure or embarrassment."

"Embarrassment? Over what?"

"Over me acting like I have another chance with you. You know…"

She does. She nods, smiling wanly. Her body seems to twitch with the impulse to lean into me.

"I'm happy to be your friend, Mary. I'd be pleased as punch for you and Pip and me to have a triangular date every day of the week. That's all I'm asking here: the three of us at my grand daughter's table for a couple of hours. Pip would like that."

"There you go again. Pip isn't inviting me. Question is: would you like it?"

"Yes. Yes, I would," I say quickly, feeling the heat rising in my face. "Very much."

I can't look at her now. I know that I am red. Peripherally, I see her smiling into the side of my face. She reads me perfectly.

"Let me tell you something, honey," she starts quietly. "I like younger men because they act like they've got a right to be considered for my bed. That thrills me – always has. The cavewoman in me, I guess. When they act that way – and temper it with a little grace, a little courtesy, a little intelligence – they usually get in. The day that an eighty-year-old bald-headed man with a gut acts that way with me is the day he gets a treat."

"I'm not bald," I snap, "and I don't have a gut."

She smiles mischievously. "Well. You've got a leg up then."

I don't like that much. I feel a little like the puny runt whom the sympathetic playground monitor has just pushed to the front of the dodge ball line. "What's the leg-up for your German boyfriend?" I ask with a deliberate edge.

She stiffens. She studies my eyes quite closely, then relaxes and chuckles. "You've still got a little mean in you, don't you, Mortie?"

"I'm just asking…"

"Well, he's not my boyfriend," she rumbles. "Not even close."

"What is he then? What's his magic that you spend all that time with him in the community room?"

She shakes her head, purses her lips thoughtfully, as if debating how much she will share with me. When she finishes shaking and pursing she says, "Karl Becker is a very long story. This much I'll tell you and then we'll never speak of him again: he and I share a war experience; he is an old associate, important to me for reasons that have nothing to do with money, friendship or romance. Can you live with knowing just that?"

I shrug. "It's not like I'm so important to you that I have to worry about it."

"Stop it," she commands. "Stop now before you trip and fall into one of your big muddy puddles of self-pity." I'm marshalling my forces for some sort of counterattack when she smiles and says, "I like this."

She pats my hand – I suspect in a patronizing way until she holds it and interlaces her fingers with mine. I can't look up at her eyes, I just can't. I keep staring at her hand, which is so beautiful and graceful and seems so out of place on a woman older than forty. She reads that thought too.

"Mayonnaise," she says lightly.

"What?"

"I wear mayonnaise gloves to bed every night that I sleep alone."

I study her face looking for a punch line. This image rises up in my brain: her in a silky half-slip and a lacey bra sitting on the edge of my bed with her hands in yellow latex gloves with mayonnaise oozing out. I finally laugh. Mary laughs and squeezes my hand a little harder. I squeeze back. She smiles a lovely intimate smile that lets me know that I'm making nice progress. The smile suddenly evaporates – she looks at her wristwatch.

"Oh, got to go right now. TAGS."

She gives me a peck on the cheek, jumps up and leaves without another word.

The touch of her lips lingers. The more I savor it, the more I think of Karl Becker. I dislike him no matter how unromantic his connection to Mary is. I don't go back to my room. I pass the fifth floor, get off on the fifteenth floor and go to the library. I get on the internet and I Google-search Karl Becker. There are a million Karl Beckers: Hitler's artillery production chief, a Roman Catholic theologian, a Chicago violin maker, a New Jersey advertising executive. Most of those people are dead already and none of them, living or dead, look anything like Mary's man. I pull down the binder of Argyll resident biographical sketches. Each Argyll resident is asked to write a one-page sketch, for posting on the lobby bulletin board when he or she first arrives. Karl Becker has no such bio sketch in the binder.

Charmaine Again

I call Charmaine back. "We're a go for a *week* from this Sunday, if that's okay with you. Mary's got something going this coming Sunday."

"Two Sundays from now is fine," Charmaine says. "We'll pick you up at Hayward BART at twelve-thirty. We'll obviously talk before then, of course. Pip can come out to you Tuesday morning?"

"Oh, God, please!"

"Great, the usual time then."

In the background I can hear Pip yelling with joy.

"But," I say, "I want you and me to have lunch this coming Monday – just the two of us."

"Mondays are incredibly busy for me at work. I've got to squeeze in a lot before

I can leave to get Pip. Remember: she's with my neighbor on Mondays, her psychiatrist day."

"This is important and too complicated for the phone. But I think that I have a permanent year-around solution to your childcare problem."

Silence at her end. She's hooked.

"We have to meet near my workplace," she says in subdued tone.

We agree to meet at one o'clock in a café in the Third Street corridor, a five-minute walk from her office. We soon hang up. I continue looking at the dead receiver with great satisfaction. I finally lay a finger on exactly why I feel so good. I had suggested a week's delay in our Sunday dinner and Charmaine had committed to it right away – had committed her beau to it without consulting him. That seems so domestic to me, so housewife-in-control-of-her-domain. I give her points. I give him a few too. I feel better about him coming into Pip's world.

Come Monday afternoon, I take a cab to Third Street. I arrive ten minutes early. Charmaine is already there, pacing the sidewalk. She looks sadly relieved, as though she has been full of a swelling hope all weekend and is finally about to get punctured in a way that relieves a great pressure on her brain.

"Well?" she says demandingly, trying to temper her emotions with a smile.

I grasp her hand and squeeze it. She is at first shocked by my touch, but a look of warm surrender comes over her – exactly the one I see in Pip's face when I am tender with her. I remember that the last time I had touched Charmaine was to shake her violently after catching her in one of her adventures as a promiscuous seventeen-year-old. Prior to that, I recall with more pain, I had not touched her with any tenderness since she was thirteen. The exact age comes to me as I rub her hand and fight back tears: *thirteen*. I realize in that moment that I had been a terrible parent to her. I don't recall all my short-comings. I just know that it's all my fault, that I somehow should have found the will to take command of her young life the way I had found the will to take command of my buddies that morning on the beach in Normandy.

"Forgive me," I hear myself say.

"For what?"

"You know. I failed you."

"You keep saying that," she says dismissively.

"I didn't have enough energy, enough, well enough patience. I had so many problems of my own that I didn't know I had or wouldn't admit to. But I should have tried harder."

"You did all right," she says half-heartedly. "But what about Pip?"

Yeah. *No time for emotional regrets, granddad*, she's telling me with that tone. *Get to the point that will make my life easier right now.*

"I don't want strangers taking care of Pip after school this fall," I declare too loudly. "And I don't want her to be a latch-key kid when she gets older."

Charmaine chuckles bitterly. "Unless I win the lottery, I don't have much of a choice, do I?"

"You do have a choice. Let Pip go to school here in San Francisco."

She looks at me funny, I think wondering whether I have slipped into senility since our last phone conversation. "We live in Hayward, granddad. She doesn't qualify for public schooling in San Francisco."

"She could live here – with me. My address would be her address for school registration purposes. I could get her into a good school with my old contacts."

"Have her *live* in an old folks' home? I'm sorry – that's what it is."

"Um hum," I say nodding, "that's exactly what it is. An old folks' home in which she would start each school day with a hot delicious breakfast and a dozen old folks patting her head in loving encouragement. Where she'd end the day with a delicious dinner, after which she'd do her homework in the beautiful Argyll library which has a fifteenth-floor view of the most beautiful city in the world – with two retired engineers to help her with her math homework and a half-dozen retired school teachers and librarians to help her with her English and geography homework. Ah, and five musicians and two retired music professors to guide her if she decides to take up piano or violin."

"You don't have a piano," she says.

"The Argyll has a Steinway Grand in the community room. And the day she tells me she wants to take up the violin is the day she gets one."

Charmaine, still skeptical, shakes her head cautiously.

I bore in. "And who cares that it's an old folks' home anyway?" I say, pretending to be offended. "She'll be in school all day with kids her own age, won't she? She doesn't see any more of her schoolmates after she goes home to her thirty-six-year-old mother in Hayward, does she? What's the difference there?"

Charmaine is casting about for counter-arguments, afraid to be optimistic.

"No difference at all," I say, driving a nail into her brain. "And you would have her on the weekends – which is the only time you really have for her anyway. And if you miss her too much during the week, you could come to the Argyll and have dinner with her – and take a cab back to work if you have to work after hours. Or you could even stay in the Argyll guest suite now and then and sleep with her in a double bed and have breakfast with her the next morning and be just a cab ride away from work. You could keep a couple of outfits in my closet."

I'm hot now, I'm rolling.

"At least one night a week, depending on her homework load, Pip will get out to the symphony or ballet, or even the opera if she develops a liking for it. Mary and I would make a little gourmand out of her – she'd know every restaurant in North Beach, South Beach and the Mission by the time she was twelve. God knows she'd be the most stylish female in San Francisco. With her under my wing, you'd have time to work extra long hours Monday through Friday."

Charmaine's big doe eyes narrow meanly. She's looking for sarcasm now, for some sort of sneering judgment. I squeeze her hand a little harder and smile.

"Yeah," I say softly, "that's exactly what I'm thinking and not saying. But I'll say it now: you'll have a little time for you and your man."

She continues searching my eyes.

"Can we be absolutely candid here?" she says coolly.

"Sure."

"You're eighty-three. You seem to be hale and hardy now but your health could fail catastrophically next month or next week, even tomorrow."

"So could yours."

She continues as if I've said nothing: "I just wouldn't want her depending on someone – emotionally I mean – who might not be there for her a month from now. She's had enough of that over the last couple of years."

I take a deep breath. I look at her and take hold of both her hands now.

"Absolutely candid, right?" I confirm.

She nods cautiously.

"When you called me back in May, you were ready to use me up Tuesday through Friday as a babysitter, right? Whether I lived one more day or one more month or six more summers, you were ready to just burn me out. Right?" I squeeze her hands hard, to squeeze the truth out of her.

"Right," she says.

"Well, what's the difference – except a happier and more scheduled situation for Pip until the day I die?"

She looks at me as if I've asked her to marry me and she doesn't know whether I'm that trustworthy. After a long moment she says: "Pip could get into a good school here?"

"Claire Lilienthal, the finest K-through-8 school in San Francisco. It's a five minute drive from the Argyll. I'd take her in the Argyll town car or in a cab every morning and Mary or I would pick her up every afternoon. That would take her through the eighth grade and fast track her for the best private high schools in the city."

Charmaine laughs. "We certainly won't have any private school money. School supplies will be a victory."

I fix her with a stare that she takes as unfriendly. That's how intense it is. "I'm setting up an education fund for her," I say. "She'll have whatever she needs. From here to Harvard, whatever she needs."

Charmaine melts. That look again but she fights it. She pulls her hands out of mine, pulls them up to her face and closes her eyes tightly. She strains for a while to keep it all in but it explodes. I move to hold her but remember that I long ago lost that privilege. All I can think of is to get us out of the stream of high-noon pedestrians flowing by staring at us. I hail a cab, just wanting to get our family business off the streets.

"We're just riding," I say to the cabbie. "Just take your time driving down the Embarcadero."

Charmaine recovers some poise but doesn't speak. She just looks out her window as we ride along. We're down around the Ferry Building before she says ever so quietly:

"I'm so sorry about grandma Dottie."

I can't say anything to that. Another long stretch of thoroughfare goes by before she says:

"2007 just wasn't a good year for me," she says. "There were four deaths that just crushed me. First, there was my ex's mother. Gloria. I loved that woman. She did so much for me, for the kids. Not just material things. She gave all of us love and respect and encouragement. She was about the only human being besides Pip who had a real relationship with Ulrich. She was the only adult wisdom in all our lives."

I swallow hard on that one. I keep looking at her as she continues looking out her window.

"I think I married my ex more to be Gloria's daughter-in-law than to be his wife. When she died, a part of me died too." She finally turns her head and looks at me. "I don't want you to laugh at this now…our pet dog got killed. Becky. A golden lab. She was really Ulrich's and Pip's dog. The two of them just adored Becky. They were a trio. They went everywhere together except to school. One time Ulrich refused to go to school for a whole week while Becky was ailing. Pip and Ulrich didn't want to make Becky choose in which of their rooms she would sleep. So, Pip and Ulrich shared a room so the three of them could be together all the time. Becky got run over. Her pelvis got crushed. We had to put her down. That was so hard on them."

Charmaine chokes on whatever words were next coming out of her. She gathers herself for a moment, then breaks a little.

"Especially on Pip!" she bursts. "Pip saw the truck hit Becky. She nearly got hit herself running out into the street to get to Becky. After I put Becky down, the two of them blamed me for killing her. They thought saving her was just a matter of money that I wasn't willing to spend. The two of them retreated so deeply into themselves. They circled their wagons so tightly that even I couldn't get in. They said if I had really loved Becky I wouldn't have let her die. I knew they would eventually understand and forgive me, so I didn't worry too much at the time. They had each other, each other and their Axis and Allies. They'd play for days. Then Ulrich's aneurysm burst one day when he and Pip were playing. It just burst and, the doctors said later, he must have just fallen where he stood and died in a matter of seconds. Pip called 9-1-1, then tried to call me. She couldn't get hold of me. I was working in Oakland at the time, for a trucking company. I was at lunch and had left my cell phone on the desk of a co-worker who had locked her office for lunch. No one could get to my phone, no one knew it was urgent. I didn't hear until I got back from lunch and by the time I rushed to the hospital, Pip had been alone essentially in the waiting room for two hours. Two hours, knowing her brother was lying dead in some room nearby. She was mute for a month after that. She would eat but she wouldn't do anything else. I was relieved when she came out of her mute shell. But when she did, she only wanted to play Axis and Allies by herself. School started and that helped her. When she excelled at school I thought she was on the road to recovery. But she stayed inside herself. She explained to me that she really wasn't concentrating in school. It was Ulrich, brilliant little Ulrich, performing for the two of them. Ulrich is always in there with her, in that little world she has created for the two of them. The three of them, including Becky. I can't get into that world. Worrying so much about Pip has sort of deferred my full grieving over Ulrich. Still, I grieve. I cry myself to sleep most nights. I'm worried to death for Pip."

"Look, I just can't drive around this long without a real destination," the cabbie interrupts.

I fish out two twenties, hand them to him and tell him to keep his damned mouth shut. A very awkward moment. Charmaine is shocked by my rudeness and for an instant I am terrified that I have broken the magic of her heartbreaking candor.

"Please," I say, almost pleading. "Don't stop."

After a long moment of looking out the window, she starts again. "One day, I'm scouring the *Chronicle*, looking for a new job – I need a job with really good health benefits because I want to get top flight psychiatric care for Pip. That's when I see grandma Dottie's photo on the obituary page. Just by accident I saw it. If I had been blinking or sneezing as I turned the pages I would have missed it. I'm sorry I didn't call. But I just couldn't take talking about one more death. I just couldn't. And after months…"

She's got no heart to continue. I'm not sure I can continue listening because my heart is cracking too. I squeeze her hand, more to anchor myself than to comfort her.

"It's all right, honey. Leave it there."

But she doesn't. She gives me one more little piece of grace: "I was just too devastated by things to call you, but I did manage to scratch out a little letter and mail it to you. When I didn't hear from you, I figured you didn't want to hear from me."

"When?" I say, shocked.

"When what?"

"When did you send this letter?"

"A few days after I saw the obituary."

"I never got that letter! I didn't get it, Charmaine!"

"No?" she says relieved.

An image arises before my eyes: that mountain of untended mail beside my front door. "Oh, Jesus Christ!" I say as I smack my forehead with my palm. "Oh, God, what am I saying? I stopped looking at the mail when Dottie died. I didn't even touch it. One day I just scooped it all up and dumped it. I am so sorry, honey. I wasn't ignoring you."

Her eyes fill. I reach out for her hand. It's a reflex, it's gratitude for her not having forgotten Dottie. Her hand is inert in mine. When I squeeze it she looks out her window again.

"When I did get around to calling you, it was months later. Your phone had been disconnected. I called Mrs. Hendricks next door to see what was happening. She told me you'd moved to this Argyll retirement community." She looks around to me with hurt in her eyes. "I called you there once. You remember answering the phone in early May, and saying hello and no one talking at the other end? Do you remember that?"

"I remember," I say. And I do. Aside from the Argyll activity director pestering with calls, no one ever called.

"That was me calling. I heard your voice – it was the first time in six years – and I just froze. I just suddenly felt all the guilt crashing down on me for being so late in reaching you, for not staying in touch, for not giving grandma Dottie the least little bit of pleasure by just sending her a note or inviting her out to lunch or remembering her birthday. The angrier you got with the silence at my end of the line, the more I froze. When you started swearing I hung up. I didn't call back that day. I couldn't summon the courage. And something about the way you talked into the silence let me know that I really had no right to call at all." She attempts a sad little smile and turns her head to look out her window again. "After a week or so, I dialed your number a couple of more times. Each time I dialed, I would remember your anger from my days in your house and I would hang up before your phone got through its first ring." She laughs after a moment. "You can imagine how absolutely desperate I was when I called and asked you to watch Pip."

Every word she has spoken has been a hammer blow to my head. But I'm stuck on *I remembered your anger from my days in your house.*

Your house. God.

I wonder if I had been an adequate father in any dimension of that term, if this odds-and-ends life which three of my direct descendants had lived was due directly to my failures. Melissa. Charmaine. Pip. I repeat their names silently. Each name is an explosion inside my brain. What else could I conclude but *No, you were a fucking shit-bag of a father! What else do these three have in common except their relationship – or lack of it when it was needed – with YOU?*

"When I called you for help," Charmaine says quietly, "I was just too ashamed of myself to bring up grandma Dottie." She bursts. Completely this time. She is crying for all the losses in her life – I feel this as I scoot over and enfold her. I feel her mother whom she had never known, the father she had never known, her husbands, her mother-in-law Gloria, Becky, Ulrich, her grandma Dottie. They all pour out of her in unrelenting torrents.

Then I burst, out of nowhere my tears pour. I'm embarrassed at first, especially so when Charmaine seems to suspend her own grief in incredulous witness of my own. I take her head in my hands and say, "We'll cry out all our grief right here, you and I. Then we'll be better, better for our living loved ones."

Her eyes go wide, like I've said something incredibly wise. Then we cry on, calling out the names of our loved ones. I shout them out, the names of war buddies as well. But my throat closes every time I try to call out Melissa's name.

My Melissa. My baby. She too had been a stranger in my angry house. *Oh, my love. I am so sorry. I am so, so sorry.*

Tick, Tick, Tick

I lie awake thinking of Charmaine's brutally frank comment on my life expectancy. I debate the wisdom of encouraging Pip to depend upon me. Her coked-out father, her paternal grandmother, her maternal great grandmother, Becky, Ulrich: do I really want to get in that queue? I remember my comeback to Charmaine's concerns, but I find her concerns more compelling. I take my pulse on my wrist and on my jugular: I guess it to be in the high-sixties. I click on the bed stand light and put on my blood-pressure sleeve. One fifty-five-over-eighty-five. Not bad for eighty-three with heart valve problems, but not good for a surrogate parent who needs to be around for five or six more very active years.

Nine, I tell myself.

I say it out loud: "Nine is what I want – not one year less."

I want to see Pip graduate from high school. That's a good objective. I envision it: her in a black robe and mortar board, coming toward my embrace with a big grateful smile on her face. Her hair is long and luxuriant. She has grown it out for her graduation picture, I suppose, or perhaps just to please me. She has her diploma in hand.

"Thanks, great granddad," she whispers as she kisses my cheek.

It's a nice vision.

But I wake up – it's not a vision at all. I've been in a full-blown-from-the-depths-of-REM dream. It's morning. I have slept right through the night. The first time in years, the first time that I can remember since the onset of Dottie's more serious health problems.

I get up and put on a sweat suit that I haven't worn in years. I don't know why I didn't throw it out when I down-sized from Paloma Street but I'm now glad to have it. It fits me well and that encourages me. I take the elevator up to the exercise center. When I walk in, the attendant Arturo looks at me like I'm an intruder.

"Oh, Mr. Willbanks!" he says excitedly when he finally recognizes me. "Haven't seen you up in here since your walk-through on the welcome tour!"

"I know," I say laughing. "Don't make me feel badly about that now."

I do all right. I diddle with the three-pound hand weights for ten minutes and I get up to five minutes on the treadmill before my heartbeat starts elevating scarily. Arturo advises me to call it a day and go down to a breakfast rich in electrolytes. I dress for breakfast, go down, and start off with two bananas and a big glass of orange juice. I'm well into butter-less oatmeal and an English muffin when Mary's old-fart German boyfriend comes in. He's unsteady on his feet. He seems a bit disoriented. He doesn't look good at all. I recall his vim and vigor when I first arrived at the Argyll. I recall his striding into the dining room like a forty-year-old ex-athlete, often without his wife in tow because she was too ill to come down. I remember running into him several times in the elevator when he was in his sweat suit and sneakers and heading up to the health center. So much decline in just five months. I continue watching him as he struggles through a simple meal of oatmeal and English muffin. His hand shakes when he brings his orange juice up to his lips.

I get very, very scared. I go back up to my place and call Kaiser to make three appointments: one for a comprehensive physical exam with my internist, another for a consultation with my urologist and a third for a consultation with my cardiologist. Their appointments secretaries all try to put me off for two or three weeks but I tell them all *now*, this coming Monday (when Pip won't be around). I deserve it: I'm old, I've paid taxes for nearly seventy years, I'm a veteran, I should move to the front of any service line in this country that I have helped finance and helped defend. I get my way. By the time I finish all that, my doorbell rings: the start of another Tuesday-through-Friday with Pip. I can tell from the ring that Charmaine is in a hurry to get to work. But I sit and listen to another cycle of rings. I pretend that the rings are fate calling me, drafting me for a mission. My mission is to live.

In the Principal's Office

It is a large office, somewhat starved of sunshine but a tastefully-appointed one, worthy of a man who is effectively the vice-superintendent of the city's school district. He doesn't keep me waiting for long. Just a few minutes after his secretary has ushered me in and offered me coffee, he comes rushing in like he's the junior subordinate late for a meeting with me.

"Wow, Mister Willbanks," he says a little breathlessly as he shakes my hand. "This is such an odd feeling – I can't tell you. I remember the time you were vice principal at Wash and you called me into your office for that first 'little chat.' Remember?"

"Oh, I remember," I say laughing.

"Sit, sit, please."

"Thank you for agreeing to see me on such short notice," I say as we both settle into chairs.

"Actually, Saturdays are pretty good days for short-notice meetings," he says. "And how could I deny you? A meeting, of all things! Those 'chats' turned my life around, as you can see. I'm in this office, rather than a jail cell, because of you."

I look around the office with him. I say: "I'm sure that any jail time you would have done can't possibly compare with the hard time you're doing here."

He laughs sincerely, turning his big desk chair in little arcs as he gives full vent to his amusement. He takes a few minutes to review his academic history and career path, several times thanking me for both. He introduces me to his fine family smiling from several framed photographs on his back credenza. As he prattles on about his children, it dawns on me that he considers me some sort of de facto godfather who is significantly responsible for the way in which they have turned out. He's in the midst of bragging about how his oldest daughter has just finished her residency in a prestigious New York hospital and is now off to work with Doctors Without Borders in Uganda. Suddenly he stops and smiles at me.

"This is probably going to embarrass you," he says a little tentatively, "but I want you to know it anyway. The way you treated me and managed me those four years we were together at Wash? That's exactly the way I've treated and managed my own children. I had no other model for what a father is supposed to be like. You were it, Mr. Willbanks. Just you."

"Wow," I say.

I'm not trying to low-ball it. It is really all I can say, I'm so stunned. He continues looking at me, his solemn gratitude becoming more intense and more evident by the second as his eyes soften and his mouth fights an urge to quiver.

"You always had a core to you, Reggie," I say, just to say something, to tamp down the drama. "You would eventually have gotten in touch with it somehow."

He laughs. "Maybe, maybe not. I'm guessing not."

When he segues to a review of my last thirty years, I get right down to business. I'm not going to wait for him to tire of my presence and then ask half-heartedly, *Now what can I do for you?*

"I have a great granddaughter who is very much at risk," I say solemnly. "She lives in Hayward now with her single and somewhat indigent mother. She's in a school environment that's going to just eat her alive over the next decade. That's just not acceptable to me because she is probably – potentially – the most brilliant and most loving human being I've ever known. For the next several years I want her to live with me here in San Francisco during the school year. I want her to attend Claire Lilienthal for the rest of her elementary and middle school years and then perhaps move on to University or Lick-Wilmerding."

He looks solemnly, admiringly, at me and puffs. "I would make that possible in a heartbeat if…"

"If…"

"If it weren't so irregular. Applications were due in March. Decisions were made in mid-May. Decision letters went out to parents in mid-June, five weeks ago now. Your great granddaughter would displace a child whose parents have already been notified of their child's acceptance at Claire Lilienthal."

"No, I don't want anyone displaced. I'm not thinking of that. There's a waiting list, right? There's always a waiting list."

He nods cautiously.

"As I recall, the first one or two percent on the list eventually get in. Accepted children fall ill, parents of accepted children get job-transferred, well-off parents decide at the last moment to go the private or home-schooling route. All I'm asking is that you place my child at the top of the waiting list. No one gets displaced."

"That also would be highly irregular."

I nod. "Almost as irregular as my not accepting a single extra penny for doing double duty as teacher and vice principal at Wash for five years – during which time I made the highly irregular decision not to report your felony to either your grandmother or the police authorities."

He blinks. I see wheels turning in his pupils. His eyes wander away from me and settle on some point behind my shoulder. He seems to think harder. He nods.

"You've got it," he finally says, as if it's a snap command decision that he's had no trouble making. "But you still have to do every page of the standard paperwork."

"I'll get it from your secretary on my way out. I'll complete it and return it to you tomorrow."

He wants to reminisce more but I've got things to do. I commit to a catch-up lunch at some later date and leave somewhat awkwardly. It hits me as I ride the elevator down: I have never before asked for grace or favor from anyone in my life. Except for Dottie's hand in marriage. Otherwise, not a single *personal* thing from anyone. *To need* had always been a basic human weakness to me. I can't recall ever using the verb *to need* regarding myself in any intimate conversation or correspondence. *Another step,* I think almost out loud. Whether a step toward a surrendering old age or toward a fuller humanity I'm not sure.

The thoughts just keep flying at me as I stand outside the school district headquarters trying to flag down a cab. That bomb finally goes off, the one that I thought I had defused in the office upstairs. *I had no other model. You were it, Mr. Willbanks.*

I break. Tears stream. So I had made a difference to someone – I hadn't messed up every young life I had touched. I think of fatherless Pip. I think of how well I was doing with her until I blew up, how close I came to losing her. I shiver.

I pull out my Blackberry. I still don't know how to use it really, but Pip has put her number on speed dial for me.

"Hello, great granddad?" I hear her ask worriedly. "Is everything all right?"

"Everything's just perfect, honey. I just miss you so much and I wanted to hear your voice."

"You don't get enough of it Tuesday through Friday?"

"Never enough, my little dove." *My little dove?* "See you Tuesday."

"Okay."

I click off. By the time a cab stops for me I can't tell it's yellow. My eyes are that full.

In the Middle of the Night

Later that night, it stings me like a mosquito's bite: that day in the cab Charmaine had said that four deaths had crushed her in 2007. Nearly a week has passed since our time in that cab but I'm sure she had gotten through just three deaths before we had disintegrated in each other's arms. Gloria, Becky, Ulrich. I think hard: I don't believe she was counting Dottie as the fourth because she said that she had been crushed by four before she knew about Dottie.

    It's nearly one in the morning. But it's early Sunday morning. She doesn't have to get up for work. I recall that Charmaine was a heavy sleeper as a child, that she returned readily to sleep after being disturbed in the night. I call.

"Hello?" she says leadenly.

"Charmaine, it's me. I'm sorry about the hour but I just have to know now, even at the risk of upsetting you. You said last week that you suffered through four deaths in 2007. You only got to three. I'm just now remembering that."

Silence. Then: "My marriage."

"What?"

"The death of my marriage. The formal dissolution degree came through last year, just about the time Gloria died. It was the death of my marriage, the death of any possibility that Ulrich and Pip would have a present father in their lives."

"I'm so sorry," I say impotently.

"Life goes on," she says wearily.

"But he can still be a part of Pip's life, can't he? I mean, the death of the marriage need not be the death of the tie between father and daughter."

"He's an addict, granddad," Charmaine says with a sort of seething patience. "He was an in-control recreational coke user by our first anniversary. He was a full-blown addict by the time we separated. He was so out of it that he didn't even show up for Ulrich's funeral." She draws a big breath to fuel a more emotional commentary on that spousal failing. She gets out an unintelligible syllable or two, abruptly stops herself and blows out the rest of her breath in a long exhausted sigh. After a long moment of silence she says in a deadened tone, "The divorce just made things so clear to me. It sort of ripped the gauze from my eyes so that I could see things for what they really were. He's lost. Lost to himself. Lost to Pip. The worst of it is that he's very comfortable with things the way they are. He thinks things are normal."

I can't help myself: "Did your…did the, the open marriage wear away at his morale?"

A long silence.

"You mean: did my fucking other men -- a black man in particular -- demoralize him and send him spiraling down into despair and drug addiction?"

I wince. I recall her foul language, recall how she would bombard Dottie and me with it as she stood in our entry way defending herself against our insistence that she tell us where she had been all night. Oh, she would go on to tell us – in a seamless stream of foul verbs and filthy details. Dottie would break and weep under the bombardment. And I would advance on Charmaine with clenched fists…

"Yes, that's what I mean," I say quietly.

"I know what you are thinking. You're thinking about my reckless youth, aren't you?

Have you ever stopped thinking about it? What: you think my name and *slut* just naturally comes to mind as a suffix?" She sighs heavily. It seems to vent all the welling bitterness. "I sought comfort with one good man," she says evenly, "one good man after years of my husband's messing around…" She stops and chuckles with a brittle edge. "He had a dozen women – a different dozen every month. It's something of an occupational hazard in the music video industry. Like the drugs. It was *me* who was in despair, granddad. Okay? *I* spiraled down. But into the arms of a loving tender man that I sent away because he was black and I was basically a social coward. When it was clear that Pip wasn't his child, I…"

"Go on," I say after a long silence. I try to make it a humble request.

Charmaine laughs bitterly. "*Go on?* You want to hear all this? You never wanted to hear anything like this before."

"Maybe I've grown a little since then."

She takes a moment, I think trying to decide whether she can trust me with more details. "I need to get to sleep. Another day for my mess of a life and for your personal growth adventures, huh?"

"Just one more question, please."

"Yes?" she says shortly.

"Why didn't you stay in touch with us? In the beginning I mean – with Dottie at least."

"I knew I had messed up in your eyes – both of you. Grandma Dottie was far less judgmental than you but still you both felt I had messed up everything. I didn't run as far as mom to get away from the judgment but that's essentially what I was doing when I married so young and so stupidly the first time. I thought I would build a home where I was treasured despite my faults. And after that…I really don't feel like pulling out the encyclopedia of my broken life right now, all right?"

"It's not broken anymore, honey," I say. "Maybe once it was. But you are doing a wonderful job of pulling it together. It takes so much strength and courage to do what you're doing. Maybe you don't see yourself succeeding because at the end of every day you are so tired and discouraged, and maybe you wake up most days tired and discouraged. But you're wonderful. Pip proves that. And Ulrich proves it – he continues to prove it through the big part of him that Pip keeps alive in her heart. And now he is in my heart too. It's all because of you. You're a great mother and a lovely woman."

The silence is crushing. It's absolute. All my words echo in the void and I feel so stupid.

"That's nice," she says, a little flatly but it exhilarates me. "That's nice, thank you for that. Good night."

"Good night, my love."

"What?" she says, suddenly very alert.

I hang up. Embarrassed. I would no more repeat that than I would let Charmaine see me naked.

Another day for all that, I think guiltlessly. I'm a recovering angry old man. I've got to take things slowly.

Paige Middleton-Palmer

"Jesus Christ," I moan. "How stupid can I possibly be?"

"Don't be so hard on yourself," Mary says. "You're charging straight ahead. Details get lost in the dust when you're charging this hard."

"Quite a significant detail, don't you think?"

It's so stupid. I've been laying plans to have Pip live with me in an old-age home that is a condo association and I hadn't stopped to think about the possibility that Argyll rules prohibit the residency of a nine-year old.

"I'm sure there's something in the CCR's that addresses the issue," Mary says. "I'm on the HOA board – I should be able to quote section and sub-section, but I can't. I imagine that the guest rule alone would trip you up."

The Argyll guest rule is that no resident can have an overnight guest for more than ten consecutive nights, and for no more than an aggregate of twenty nights in any three-hundred-sixty-five-day span of time.

"For what it's worth, Mortie: if there's any wiggle room in the CCR language, you have my full support on the board in exploiting it."

"What are the chances of wiggle room, huh?" I say glumly. "I'm so stupid. And I've gotten Charmaine and Pip so excited over this."

"Just check it out first before you mention anything to them," Mary says, squeezing my hand sympathetically. "You need to consult a good lawyer. Know of any?"

I shake my head.

"I know a good one. I'm not sure she does condo association stuff but she's the world's best corporate-law litigator. I mean she's the proverbial eight-hundred-pound gorilla stomping on ant hills in the jungle clearing. She charges a thousand dollars an hour and is super busy, but I'm sure that I can get you a little pro bono time. Shall I set something up for you?"

"For me alone? You won't be there?"

She smiles. "No. I want you to meet her the first time by yourself. Get to know her through your own inter-personal efforts and observation."

"Jesus, Mary, I'm looking for a lawyer, not a bride."

"This is, in addition to being part of your Pip agenda," she says smiling, "a stretching exercise for you." She reaches across the table and pats my hand. "Trust me here."

Mary has got some sort of pull with this lawyer. Mary calls her at her home at noon on Sunday and gets me a fifteen-minute appointment for the very next afternoon. The lawyer asks us to courier a copy of the Argyll CCR's to her office early Monday morning. Paige Middleton-Palmer is her name. My Google research tells me that she is one of the Connecticut Middletons of colonial and revolutionary-era fame. The Middleltons who quintupled their traditional fortune by brokering Middle Eastern oil deals between the world wars. The law firm of Middleton, Bryce and Cameron is a big player in the Ecuador versus Chevron environmental disaster litigation.

"How do you know her?" I ask Mary.

"Oh, my, where to begin?" she says. "Short version of the answer is that she and I serve on the board of the non-profit that runs the halfway house for TAGS."

"I'm getting the feeling that your life is full of long versions to things."

"Yeah," she says, nodding thoughtfully. "That it certainly is."

Middleton, Bryce and Cameron are near the top of the 101 California building, *the* top-drawer office tower in San Francisco. The building directory features eight-hundred-pound-gorilla names: Merrill Lynch, Booz and Company, Deutsche Bank, Morgan Stanley. I'm shown into Paige's empress-of-the-world office with its panoramic view of the Bay, the Embarcadero and the bridges. I am told to take a seat, she'll be right in. It's the fifth office in two weeks that I've been shown into and told to wait: the school district administrator, my internist, a local child psychiatrist, my urologist and now this world-beating corporate litigator. I'm restless, still discouraged by my legal situation at the Argyll and I just can't sit. I walk around her office looking at the diplomas and the art work. She too has a credenza populated by portrait photos of family members. A husband, two sons, two daughters. They are sinfully good-looking Anglo-Saxons who smile out at a world that they seem to own. *Except* for one shy dark-skinned girl who has no portrait photo but who smiles out meekly at the world in a family group photo. I move closer to the credenza and squint intently. The girl appears to be about Pip's age, in any case too young to be a maid. Adopted? A strikingly attractive middle-aged woman, whom I take to be Paige, stands behind the girl and embraces her with both arms. The white siblings of the portrait photos flank her and smile their affirmations of general domestic happiness.

The girl is not only dark-skinned. I see now that she is definitely African.

A rich do-gooder family, I think, but not unkindly so.

Paige Middleton-Palmer glides into the room, all warm graciousness, string of pearls and elegant knit suit.

"Good afternoon, Mr. Willbanks," she says, smiling at my hands.

It is only then that I realize that I've picked up the photo frame with the African girl in it.

"My youngest daughter Yovanna," Paige says, so confident in her perceptive brilliance. "We adopted her two years ago. She was born in Zimbabwe."

"She seems very bright," I say, just to say something.

Paige pauses, smiles faintly, averts her eyes momentarily. "She isn't," she says matter-of-factly. "She has significant developmental issues. But she is beautiful." She tentatively takes the frame from me and smiles brightly at it. "She won't let us take any portrait photos of her. She's very shy and thinks that a portrait photo would highlight her condition." She replaces the frame on the credenza. "One day though," she says in a rather wistful tone. "Have a seat, Mister Willbanks. Let's sit over here and enjoy the view."

She leads me to a conversational island defined by a large African tribal rug, a small glass table with a laptop on it and three cane chairs. Her big picture window frames a vignette that belongs on the cover of some chamber of commerce magazine. Cars and trucks whiz into the City along the upper deck of the Bay Bridge; the Golden Gate Bridge glows orange in its afternoon majesty; sailboats flit and scud to avoid a huge cargo ship surging toward the setting sun outside the straits; airliners converge on queuing streams flowing down to the runways of Oakland Airport. All of this under a clear blue sky that seems so intimate as to envelop the world like a low-flung tent top.

"On a really clear day, when the atmospherics are just right," Paige says, "you can just about see the vineyards in Sonoma."

This is Pip's world, I think suddenly, a propos of absolutely nothing. *One day she will inherit all of this and make it so much better.*

"I've reviewed the CCR's and the addendum of house rules," Paige Palmer says.

"Already?" I say shocked. "You just got those this morning."

"The promptest of service for friends," she says with a wan smile. "Anyway, your situation is quite straightforward. In my opinion, you are on firm legal ground in moving your great granddaughter into the Argyll. The core issue for those who would dispute your right to do so is that the CCR's do not robustly define the term 'guest.'"

"And that's my 'firm legal ground?'" I say laughing nervously.

"Amani cannot possibly be classified as a 'guest' if three conditions simultaneously prevail. A: she is directly related to you by blood; B: and this is most important -- she is *exclusively* your financial dependent; and C: she lives in the Argyll Tower community in a manner consistent with permanent resident status in the City of San Francisco. Regarding A: can you lay hands on the birth certificates of your daughter Melissa, your granddaughter Charmaine and of Amani?"

Amani. Hearing it a second time from the thin lips of a Connecticut Yankee power attorney somehow, I am ashamed to say, legitimizes it. It imparts a certain gravitas that I have denied it.

"I surely can," I say. "I've kept Melissa's and a certified copy of Charmaine's in a bank safe deposit box for decades. I'm sure that I can get Amani's from Charmaine within the week."

"Regarding B: can you arrange with Amani's mother to have Amani become your financial dependent for school-expense, health insurance and federal income tax purposes?"

"No problem."

Paige leans back in her chair and studies me with unblinking frankness. After a long moment she says, "If you were ever quizzed on your commitment to Amani – by a neighbor in the elevator or by an attorney in a court proceeding – it would work to your advantage if you were able to say that Amani is not only your financial dependent but your very reason for living. Would you feel comfortable in making that sort of emotional declaration?"

I am silent for quite a long time – I'm sure that Paige misinterprets the silence. I realize that the declaration she seeks has been at the very core of my being for weeks now. It has been so *there* that it has been unnecessary to think about it, like it being unnecessary to ponder whether one will inhale the next breath of oxygen. Now that Paige has articulated the question I just want to sit here and savor the answer.

I come forward in my chair toward her. I say: "I love Amani with all my heart, breath and soul. She's mine. That's it." Paige smiles, nods. "Regarding C: Amani should eat at least sixty per cent of her meals in the Argyll dining facility, month by month."

"Done."

"Further regarding C: in addition to her nine-month-a-year attendance at Claire Lilienthal, you should enroll Amani in some sort of academically-oriented summer program in San Francisco. This would cement her status as a year-around student resident."

"I don't want to burn her out on school," I say cautiously.

"I understand." She looks away from me and out the picture window. She seems lost in her world for long seconds but she comes back to me with a snap smile. "Tell me. What does Amani love to do? What would she work hard at for six hours on summer days and not even realize that she's working hard?"

"Well, she likes math."

Paige Palmer laughs. "No one likes math *that* much."

We both laugh.

"Ah!" I exclaim. "Fashion design. That's her passion. But that's not very academic, is it?"

"Fashion design," Paige echoes faintly, impressed.

"You should see some of her stuff. It really is marketable. Mary is going to get some of Pip's – Amani's – stuff in front of her old associates in New York."

Paige leans back in her chair and studies me for a few seconds. Suddenly she comes forward and starts punching into the laptop on the table.

"I may have something for you there," she says. "I have a friend who used to serve on the advisory board of the San Francisco Art Institute. Let me just see if she's still there... Yes. Yes, she is. The Institute itself would have nothing for a child that young, but my friend would know the universe of local possibilities for young people. I'll give her a call and get back to you."

"Thank you," I say, nearly breathless with gratitude.

"If you and Mary have time and financial wherewithal, you might consider taking Amani to the summer program at the Toronto Design Exchange. It's a developmental hotbed for talented pre-teens. And Toronto is a wonderful summer vacation town. If you can get just one of her pieces into a for-profit clothing store, she will shoot to the top of the applications pile."

More opportunities for Amani. But I'm stuck on the *If you and Mary*. That sounds so good, so normal. I feel my face warming.

"Thank you for the tip," I say humbly.

She smiles at me. Belatedly I realize that it's a *Yeah, that's right, we girls have been talking about you* sort of look that Dottie's girlfriends used to give me in the honey days of our marriage.

"Excellent," Paige says. "I think that we are done for the day. Get me photocopies of the three birth certificates, have that conversation with your granddaughter regarding Amani's dependent status, and I'll draft an opinion letter that you can keep in your pocket and pull out if the association board gives you a hard time."

"Are you available to represent us if it comes to a lawsuit?"

"I am. But it won't come to that. The HOA board will no doubt re-write the rules to prohibit the future residency of young children. But, in order to avoid a lawsuit *from you*, the board will grandfather Amani in."

"Well, great-grandfather her in."

Paige laughs, I think sincerely. It's only my third weak attempt at wit in I don't know how many years and I feel flattered.

Two good-looking babes think I'm funny.

"That's great," I say. "This is all just great."

She stands up, offers me her hand and an exceptionally gracious smile which is nonetheless final and meant to dismiss me for the day. "Pleased to have met you, Mr. Willbanks."

"And I you, Mrs. Middleton-Palmer."

I'm at the door when she says, "That's such a sweet pet name."

I'm confused, I have no idea what she's talking about.

"Pip," she says brightly, as if the one word should make everything clear to me. "Mary says it really suits her."

"Suits her how?"

"The *Great Expectations* Pip, right? Smart. Sensitive. Loving. Vulnerable. At sixes-and-sevens as far as her parent-care is concerned… Not close?"

"Dead on," I say.

"Did her father or her mother give her the name?"

"Her mother, I'm pretty sure." Memories suddenly slice into my brain, as if they are sovereign entities independent of me and flying in from some distant place. I am momentarily stunned by the weight and the violence of their impact – I actually strain to keep my balance as I stand flat-footed at Paige's door. "I…" She frowns expectantly. "I…I used to read to her at bedtime, when she was young. Dickens was her favorite."

She nods. It's a knowing nod.

"Thank you again," I say humbly as I close the door on her.

On the elevator going down I marvel at my blasted old man's memory. How could I have remembered so many of Charmaine's teen-age delinquencies and forgotten the sweeter moments of her early years? How could I have forgotten the light and wonder in those huge doe eyes as I made Mrs. Joe and Magwitch and Estella and Pip come alive for her in her darkened room?

"Light some candles, granddad," she had ordered one night when she was about nine years old. "Turn off the electric lights and read to me by candlelight. They only had candles back then, didn't they?"

I shiver now with another recollection: I laughed at her – *made fun of her* -- when she cried over the death of Miss Havisham. I apologized soon thereafter, but she was never as tender-hearted with me after that.

I am such an ass. I have always been such a big fat ass. I bang my head against the elevator wall in belated penitence.

Prognosis

"Well," the cardiologist says, drawing out the one word, "the good news is that you're only slightly worse off now than you were ten months ago."

"That's the good news?" I laugh.

"The bad news is that you forfeited a chance to get a lot better by blowing off the diet and exercise regimen we agreed upon ten months ago."

"I know. I know. Give it to me again. I'm going to take it deadly seriously this time."

"I've heard that before, Mort. Look, this is no laughing matter."

"I'm laughing because I like living a whole lot more now. Was I laughing last time I was here?"

She studies me as she thinks. She looks down at her file on me and flips through a few pages. "Attitudinal changes are as critical as changes in lifestyle. What has changed?"

"New people in my life now. I want to enjoy them with some measure of health and consciousness for as long as I can. Listen, Doc, is Viagra absolutely out of the question at my age?"

"Oh, *that* sort of new life," she says grinning. "I see, I see. Well, good for you. It's not your age that precludes it. It's the condition of your heart. In your present condition, you'd probably die of a heart attack the first time you took it and tried something strenuous. But let's give it a year. You get on that regimen and stick to it –"

"I can't wait a year."

She leans back in her chair and fixes me with a smiling stare. "Congratulations, Morton. Welcome back."

"Thanks. It's good to be back."

Her eyes sweep over me as if seeing me for the first time. She shakes her head with emphatic finality and says, "No, we won't risk it until I see substantial improvement. However, there are certain homeopathic alternatives to Viagra, and certain natural supplements which may get you to where you want to be before I'm willing to write a prescription for Viagra."

She begins to write on a large Post-It pad. "I'm going to have you see Doctor Howard Huang. He's not in the Kaiser system. He doesn't take insurance of any type and he is very expensive. He has two offices, the main one being in Chinatown. But you would probably be more comfortable in his office near Union Square. You know the 490 Post Street building?"

"Boy, do I," I say, thinking of Dottie's numerous visits there.

"I'm giving you here the contact information for both offices."

"Can you vouch for his record of success?"

She smiles faintly. "Dozens of seventy-year-old Chinese men with young wives and young children. Not necessarily a good thing, but…" She shrugs and comes forward to hand me the Post-It. I look at it. I look up at her.

"Which office do those seventy-year-old Chinese fathers go to?"

She laughs so honestly and so infectiously that I laugh too.

"Doc, give me a straight answer for once. With all my issues, do I stand a chance of lasting ten more mobile active years?"

She smiles and shakes her head. "I can't handicap it for you, Morton. You might remain reasonably stable on your present plateau of health for a good ten years. Or you might be dead before Christmas. You know? What I've just said to you is true for everyone on the planet, including me."

"Nice cop-out," I mutter with a wink.

"Listen to me here. You just listen. You plan for a long future, *and* enjoy every single day as if it's your last. That's really all that any of us mortals can do."

"Doctor Wainwright and Doctor Lacksmi said the same thing in almost those identical words. Did you guys rehearse just for me, or is that Standard Bedside Manner One-oh-One?"

She breaks into another of her glorious grins as she writes a final note in my file and closes it. "Wisdom is wisdom, whatever its source. You just take it and run with it as far as you can."

Charmaine Again

When I return to the Argyll after visiting the doctor, Charmaine is sitting in the lobby reception area. I panic at first, thinking that today is not a Monday but a Pip day and that I have somehow messed up a rendezvous. Charmaine reads my terror perfectly as she stands to greet me.

"No, you're okay," she laughs. "Today is your day off."

"Where's Pip?"

"Having her regular Monday in Hayward: the psychologist and a play date with our neighbor."

"Why are you here?"

"Well, don't sound so glad to see me," she says with false pique.

"Sorry. I guess I'm still scared over maybe having messed up something. But everything is all right?"

"It will be when we finish. Could we just walk around the block? I've got to get back pretty soon."

"Sure."

We are just a few paces outside of the Argyll gates when she says, "One thing above all others you tried to drum into me when I was young: always tell the truth; always be truthful in your feelings and motives with others."

"Wow," I say with a chuckle. "That is such a distant echo – me trying to be a real parent."

"You said to me that I would have been willing to use you up, to burn you out as Pip's babysitter."

"That was a little rough."

"It's true. That's how desperate I was. I want to thank you for taking most of the desperation out of my life. Thank you for that."

"You are so welcome, honey."

I am so moved that I grab her hand. She looks at our joined hands with flesh-cutting neutrality, as if she's just watching a gnat crawl on her skin for a few seconds before she squashes it.

"Here's the heart of my agenda for the day, granddad," she says evenly as she disengages. "This is where the honesty comes in.

I don't want you to think that I'll ever really love you. I'll always be so incredibly grateful to you – grateful beyond words, really. But we've got too much of a past, you and I. I can't get over that past. I try to push it back but it's always there. I just can't get over what I think was your incredible cruelty and basic indifference. I know that's so cruel in itself to say so late in our lives, with you doing so incredibly much for Pip. But I don't want to feel like a manipulative hypocrite when we're together. I don't want to feel like I'm putting on a happy face with you just to get more for my daughter."

"It's okay, honey. It's all okay."

"Just let me finish this. When we were in the cab that day and we broke down in each other's arms, I must have seemed tender and loving and forthcoming. I just want to be truthful about things. I was draining several wounds, to use your words. I think at that moment I would have collapsed in anyone's arms. I just don't want you to think that all that started something special between us. Draining wounds has brought me no closer to forgiving you or loving you. God, I sound like such an ungrateful bitch."

"No, no, honey, don't do that to yourself. Don't." I can't help myself: I throw an arm around her and pull her into me. She lets me. After several long silent paces, I ask, "Are you saying all of this to hurt me?"

"No," she says, somewhat alarmed.

"You're saying it so that we can have a clean relationship on honest terms?"

"Yes."

"Then everything you've said is good, honey. Every single word of it is so clean and so pure and so good. I've destroyed so much in my life. I know that. I can't make it good. I can't. I look back to remember because some of it was good. But if I look back to analyze I'll just fall apart. Now that I know how things could have been, I would just…No, I can't look back. Forgive me for that. If you can. Thank you for letting me do something now. That's enough for me. God, to have you need me and for you to let me help you is going to complete my sorry life as much as it can be completed. That's so much more than I have any right to expect."

She stops. She turns to me fully and studies me frankly. There is no emotion in her. I am tempted to do what I always do: dial back the intensity of the moment by saying something stupid. But I decide to hang in there, to keep my mouth shut and just stand there and look squarely at her and take the heat. I pass my time in Purgatory by counting slowly. I abruptly stop at four – *Stand there and take it, you fool! Stop counting! Stop running!*

She finally blinks, sighs. "Where is Grandma Dottie buried?"

I shake my head in confusion. "What?"

"Where is Grandma Dottie buried?"

"In Colma. Cypress Lawn. Why?"

"Pip wants to visit her. She's been asking a lot of questions about Grandma Dottie, questions that I guess she's afraid to ask you for fear of hurting you in some way. We'll probably drive out there this Sunday. Maybe you can draw up a little map, so that we can find her."

"I'd rather take you to her."

Charmaine thinks a long moment. "Yeah. Yeah, that would be nice. Let's firm things up later in the week." She urgently looks at her watch, jerks her head suddenly toward the street and shoots out a hand – "Taxi!"

A taxi decelerates violently and swerves to the curb. I open the door. She gets in. As she is settling in and adjusting her skirt she says,

"Seven o'clock tomorrow morning?"

"You've got it."

She gives the driver her destination. The cab pulls away. She does not bother to look back.

The New Death Watch

I don't wait for death these days. It seeks me out though. Now and then I feel it trying to invest my kidneys, snatch at my heart. But I push it off. I pick up the pace on my dawn patrols. I attend the Argyll's seven o'clock tai chi classes with Mary. Mary says tai chi and deep-breathing exercises are the reasons you see so many really old Chinese people. (I told this to my comedienne of a cardiologist who then informed me that the reason you see so many old Chinese is because there are billions of Chinese to begin with.) I'm up to ten pounds on hand weights and I can go a thirty-one-minute mile on the treadmill. Pip has become a little dictator with Ulrich's stop watch. She times me in everything that I do. On the days

I don't feel like doing a thing, she'll click the stopwatch and stick it right in my ear and say,

"That's *our* time ticking away, great granddad. You're wasting it."

Pip's pushing me to live as long as I can – at least until she's in college, she says with a grim sort of humor. Every time she says it she reminds me of another conversation on death from some sixty-odd years ago. I think about that conversation every night as I try to fall asleep. Sometimes I dream the conversation line by line. I'm lying in a slit trench outside some village in Belgium, not far from Bastogne. It's December 1944. It's so freezing cold that our hands stick to the metal of our rifles. For a little extra insulation we wrap strips of blankets around our frozen boots. We're holding a line that we've been told must not break. The higher-ups have it in their heads that all of western civilization will be lost if we give way. My slit-trench neighbor is my good buddy Eddy Petrocelli from the Bronx. We have survived Omaha Beach together, fought through Saint Lo and raced across France side-by-side. We think ourselves lucky to have gotten this far in the war with just scrapes and flesh wounds and no trench foot. The Germans are not eighty yards away. They sound closer in the pitch darkness. We hear their tanks rumbling up for a morning assault. We know that they outnumber us ten to one and that we have neither reinforcements nor air support coming before their advance. They start lofting mortars at irregular intervals, to keep us sleepless and on edge so that we will be exhausted when the morning's fight begins. A mortar lands in a close-by slit trench. Blood and warm offal rain down on us.

"Who was it?" someone shouts out.

"Joel!" somebody shouts back. "They got Joel!"

Silence. We all love Joel Levy. Joel is the most selfless and courageous of us. He's the only one who seems to know what this war is really about. And he's the only one of us who has a real wife waiting for him back home.

Then some asshole off to the left of us shouts, "We're all gonna die tonight! Every fucking one of us is going to die!" He starts bawling like a wet baby. He's been sent to the front from some cushy chauffeur's job for a three-star general and he has already lost his mind.

"No!" Eddy shouts out. "No more of us die tonight! Not one fucking more! And no one dies tomorrow! We've all got to live long enough to save the world tomorrow! That's it! Nobody else dies until the world is saved!"

Somewhere out in the darkness a German who understands English has heard Eddy, and laughs loud enough for us to hear him. We laugh too finally, but we take Eddy seriously somehow. We huddle down in our slit trenches and grit our teeth through the cold and the mortar shells.

The next day, we stop the Germans cold. Against tanks and ten-to-one odds, we just plain kick their asses. It's like Pip rolling nothing but ones and twos for eight defending infantry units. Each of us in those frozen trenches plays his part on the day of battle and not one of us dies that day. The day *after* the battle is a different story. Two guys get shot in an ugly episode of friendly fire. Two more are crushed when their jeep skids off a frozen road and overturns in a ditch. Eddy steps on a mine – one of ours we're pretty sure.

But Eddy had been right. *Tomorrow* had been much too important a day on which to die and no man who understood the importance of *Tomorrow* had allowed himself to die on that day.

And that's what I say every night that I turn out the lights with Pip curled up on the sofa bed missing Ulrich, looking forward to another soothing day with Mary and me: *Not Tomorrow,* I say to all the gods of death. *The next day, maybe. But not Tomorrow.*

I speak the words out loud now. I don't realize how loudly until I hear Pip say leadenly from the living room,

"Wha cha say, great granddad?"

"Nothing," I say as gently as I can without shouting. "Go back to sleep, hon."

I get up and go to the edge of the living room, to see if she has managed to slip back into sleep. She is already snoring. A heavy sleeper she is, just like her mother. Just like her grandmother. And her great grandma Dottie, now that I think about it. I check the thermostat. I tip-toe to the sofa bed and adjust the blankets on her. I can't help myself: I sit lightly on the edge of the bed and stare at her. Gently I squeeze her little hand. I am only squeezing her hand but in my mind I am fully embracing her. I am lifting her right off the floor and crushing her to me and her feet are just dangling in the air. I am embracing my Dottie at the same time. And Mary. I embrace Melissa and hold her tight – God, so tightly I hold my Melissa. My Brad too – in all his twenty-four years I had never once told him that I loved him. Charmaine. Dear Ulrich. My arms are so long and so strong, in desperation as much as in love. I embrace Pip's father and pray for his recovery. I even embrace Paul Castlerock and pray that God's grace rain down upon him in a never-ending shower and that he become a loving influence in Pip's life. I pray that Charmaine find love and support in Paul and that she find the energy to enjoy her motherhood.

I feel so right praying these things, like it's up to me to make them happen, like I can make them happen, the way Eddy made things happen in Belgium.

It's hard to believe that I'm really awake. I sit there in the darkness full of surprise that I can think of Joel and Eddy and a hundred eighty-two others without quaking or crying out. But I am awake. My eyes are dry. My heart is calm. My head is clear.

I squeeze Pip's hand a little harder, to assure myself that she is real, that she has always been real, that I'm not already dreaming.

"Oh, Becky!" Pip suddenly whimpers in her sleep.

There is such ache in her little voice. I squeeze her hand more urgently. I open my arms a little wider and I embrace Becky too.

Other Fiction by Kenneth Aslanian-Williams (Available on Amazon.com)

Quiet Shelter in a Harbor of Friends

15 Items or Less

Made in the USA
San Bernardino, CA
18 January 2014